"I'm to scream for help,"

Courtney threatened. "I have to get out of this hospital and cut out one hundred paper picture frames. I'm the president of the Tri Beta sorority, and a lot of people are depending on me!"

The boy finally let her wriggle away from him and held her at arm's length. "Gee," he marveled, staring right into her eyes. "You're crazy."

"You're the crazy person. Go back to your ward."

"I'm not from a ward," he said, starting to crack a smile. "My name is Phoenix Cates. I'm a freshman at U. of S. I'm also your orderly. My job is to make sure you stay in bed, and I'm not going to let you out of my sight."

Don't miss these books
in the exciting FRESHMAN DORM
series

FRESHMAN SCHEMES

LINDA A. COONEY

HarperPaperbacks

A Division of HarperCollinsPublishers

HarperPaperbacks *A Division of* HarperCollins*Publishers*
10 East 53rd Street, New York, N.Y. 10022

Cover art by Tony Greco

First printing: May 1991

Printed in the United States of America

HarperPaperbacks and colophon are trademarks of HarperCollins*Publishers*

10 9 8 7 6 5 4 3 2 1

One

....

Every time sorority rush rolled around, Courtney Conner got the feeling that something extraordinary was going to happen. She'd gotten the feeling during fall rush, even though nothing special had ended up happening. But now it was spring. The whole University of Springfield campus smelled like wild flowers, and the snow atop the surrounding mountains was melting. That something-incredible-is-going-to-happen feeling was there again, and Courtney couldn't ignore it.

She approached the edge of Mill Pond, an

old logging area on campus that had been turned into a lake for swimming and paddling canoes. On this bright morning all the sororities had taken over the pond. Each house was making an elaborate float on a canoe as a way of promoting their sisterhood.

"Hi, Courtney!" called a pretty freshman, who was rushing Courtney's sorority. "You look beautiful as usual."

Courtney smiled and looked down at her red gabardine skirt and white, silk blouse. Like all the other girls, she was immaculately dressed. Rush was the time when new girls were selected by campus sororities. It was a week of traditions and rigid rules, and one of those rules was to look terrific at all times. "Thanks. Are you already finished with our float?"

"Well, we're almost done, but we need more tape, so I'm going to the campus store. See you in a little while."

Courtney smiled and walked closer to the pond, taking in all the rush activity on the main dock. Girls chattered softly. They sewed and tacked and took breaks to check their makeup. The Gammas were putting up a float with a sports theme, and the Alpha Delta

Omegas were doing something with rope and pieces of felt. Although both floats were coming along, Courtney had seen it all before.

Stalling among the crowd of overdressed, excited girls, Courtney thought back to her freshman year. She was a junior now, and even though she was president of the Tri Betas, the most prestigious sorority at U. of S., she could still remember her freshman rush so clearly that it made her tremble all over again. Rush was a grueling week where girls had to attend parties and interviews, open houses, and special events to promote the Greek system—like that morning's float parade. The rushees were checking out the various sororities, deciding which one they might want to join. More importantly, the sororities were keeping a keen eye on the girls, deciding who they wanted to ask to pledge. The week ended with the final selection of pledges and a big welcome party for the new girls.

"Courtney!" Diane Woo suddenly cried, appearing from behind the boathouse. She ran across the dock to give Courtney a rather frantic hug. A bright, dark-haired beauty, Diane was the Tri Beta's secretary and Courtney's second-in-command. She was usually the essence of efficiency and calm. "I'm so glad you're here!"

"I wasn't about to stay away," Courtney said, looking around for the Tri Beta canoe and wondering why Diane looked a little crazed. "Where are our girls?"

"On the other side of the dock," Diane said, biting her lip.

"Is something wrong?"

Diane sighed. "A couple of freshman girls who aren't rushing have been helping out with our canoe. I tried to tell them it wasn't a good idea, but they didn't want to listen."

"Who are they?" Courtney asked, following Diane past the Theta canoe, which was being decorated to look like a pale, skinny whale. Technically rush was only for girls who were trying to get into a sorority. Courtney wondered why girls would want to intrude into the rigid rush customs if they weren't interested in joining.

Diane suddenly broke into a run. "I don't know them. You decide what to do. I'll just run ahead and tell everyone that you're here."

"Okay." Courtney hurried across the dock, past piles of poster board and a bucket of felt-tipped pens. When she took another step and came around the corner of the boathouse, Courtney gasped and brought her hands to her face. Finally she sensed that this rush might be special after all.

"KC!" Courtney cried, staring at rushee KC Angeletti, and KC's two non-sorority friends.

"Hi, Courtney!" KC said.

"Yo, Madame President. What do you think?" grinned KC's friend, Winnie Gottlieb.

The third of their trio, Faith Crowley, spoke up, too. "We just wanted to help KC. I hope you don't mind."

"Mind?" Courtney repeated. She began to laugh. The Tri Beta canoe had been made to look like an old-fashioned sailboat. Two wooden frames held blue bed sheet sails, on which clouds had been painted, aloft, while orange streamers and silver tinsel pinned to the wood fluttered in the cool breeze.

"What do you think?" asked KC.

"It's beautiful," Courtney whispered.

"I know we weren't supposed to help, but we're a trio," Winnie explained. "The three of us stick together. We can't help it. We went to high school together; we're here at college together; we hang out together, fight together, cry on each other shoulders and all that corny stuff. It's bad enough that we live in separate dorms. Not that we'll all be moving into your sorority house, or anything—don't worry about that. But we had to help KC. Do you know what I mean?" Winnie threw her head back and yelled to the sky. "DOES ANYONE EVER KNOW WHAT I MEAN?"

Faith patted her shoulder. "Yes Winnie, everyone always knows what you mean." She stuck her hands in her overall pockets and smiled at Courtney. "I hope this is okay, Courtney. They let me borrow some stuff from the theater arts department, since I'm a theater major." Faith put her arms around Winnie and KC. "We just wanted to help."

Courtney wanted to cry. KC Angeletti was the one freshman rushing the Tri Betas that Courtney really wanted to become a member of her house. Even though the other rushees hanging around the canoe were richer and better connected, KC was exactly the kind of girl Courtney wanted as a "sister." Recently KC had given up going to a fancy charity ball with Courtney because Winnie had needed help. The three of them enjoyed the kind of friendship that Courtney only dreamed about.

"Anyway," Winnie chattered, shaking a half

a dozen bracelets down her arm and stomping her boots, which were decorated with bells. "We're about done. So maybe Faith and I will crawl back to our dorm rooms and leave the rest of all this ooga booga rush stuff to you experts."

"What Winnie means," Faith clarified, "is that we had a good time working on this. But we both missed some classes last week, and we have to go back to our rooms and study."

"I understand," Courtney said. As much as she admired their loyalty, she knew it was right for KC to be the only one rushing the Tri Betas. After all, Winnie was too offbeat. Her short, spiked hair, electric-blue tights and leopard print jumper weren't exactly up to sorority dress code. And Faith seemed so easygoing and artsy that Courtney couldn't imagine her worrying about her hair.

But KC was another story. She was beautiful and driven, a business major with perfectly coiffed, long dark hair who always dressed stylishly. No one would have guessed that her parents were hippies, who ran a small town health food restaurant.

Courtney looked around at the other rushees, then back at KC, Winnie, and Faith. She would have liked Winnie and Faith to hang around, but she could only bend the rules so far. "Thanks for your help. I hope to see you both again soon."

Winnie saluted and Faith smiled. They both hugged KC before turning around and starting back to the dorms.

Courtney watched them go. Then she smiled at KC, and looked down, noticing that Winnie had dropped an earring on the dock. Courtney picked it up, dangling the plastic dinosaur with purple rhinestone eyes.

"Winnie!" Courtney called, holding the dinosaur earring up in the air.

Winnie and Faith stopped, while Courtney hurried over to them. She walked briskly across the wooden dock, carefully dodging the Gamma canoe which was being carried by six girls in high heels. One of the Gamma girls started to lose her balance, though, and Courtney swerved to avoid her. The next thing Courtney knew, her high heel was stuck between two planks and her ankle had started to turn.

"Ahhhh," Courtney heard herself shout, as the heel on her shoe snapped off. Her body tipped, and before she could grab on to anything, her head smacked against something sharp and metallic. As if in slow motion, Courtney watched the pond water about to engulf her.

"Hellllllllllp!" she managed, before her shoulder plunged into the cold water. She gasped. Water pressed against her face and swept over her head. She could feel her hair floating upward, but her body only wanted to sink deeper. She struggled hard, but when she finally came to the surface, it was only for a moment. Instead of air, she swallowed another gulp of thick pond water. She could feel her mind giving away to panic. Courtney wasn't even sure now if she knew how to swim.

"Someone help her! It's Courtney Conner."

"I think she hit her head on a canoe!"

"Who has a bathing suit?"

"I can't get my shoes untied."

"Can someone help me get this silk jacket off?"

Courtney felt as if she were in the middle of a hallucination. She heard the voices while her eyes blurred and her head screamed with pain. She flailed with her arms but the water overtook her.

"Are you all just going to stand here?"

"Come on!"

"One, two, three . . . JUMP!"

Courtney heard three splashes and even though her thoughts were muddled, she somehow knew it was KC, Faith, and Winnie. They had been the only ones to jump in after her.

A moment later, Courtney was surrounded by air and she saw Faith's caring face, KC's gray eyes, and Winnie's wild wet hair. Finally, she was pulled out of the water by the three girls and set gently on the dock.

"Courtney, are you all right?" KC cried.

"Someone get a doctor," wailed Faith.

"Forget the doctor!" Winnie yelled. "Somebody take her to the hospital."

The last thing Courtney thought about before she passed out was that spring rush was turning out to be special after all.

Two
....

"**H**ow do I look?"

"Like Dash Ramirez."

"Lauren, I'm supposed to be going undercover on fraternity row. You're supposed to say that I look just like a frat brat."

"Dash, you look the way you always look— which is pretty good, if you ask me."

"Don't get fresh."

"Don't tell me I can't get fresh. Newspaper reporters are supposed to have big mouths."

"Lauren, I'm shocked," Dash joked. "And

after all the effort your rich, proper mother put into your upbringing."

Lauren laughed. "Isn't it nice when people can undergo a change?"

Dash smiled, bumped her with his hip, then leaned over his messy editorial desk at the on-campus office of the U. of S. *Weekly Journal.* In a clean, white T-shirt and new jeans, he had undergone a change, too. Usually he was covered with ink and wore a bandanna around his long, dark hair. Still, clean T-shirt or no clean T-shirt, he would never pass for a frat brat when they went to investigate their story on Greek Row.

Lauren Turnbell-Smythe, however, had been part of the sorority scene. Her mother had insisted that she rush Tri Beta that past fall, and because of her parents' generous donation, the elite sorority had accepted her as a pledge. Lauren knew, however, that they didn't really want her to join. She wasn't slim and glamorous enough to ever fit in, so she had finally gotten the nerve to quit, and overnight her whole life had turned around. Her mother had cut her off financially, forcing Lauren to take a maid's job at a downtown motel. Still, Lauren felt freer than ever. She could continue living happily in Coleridge Hall, the creative arts dorm, where she roomed with Faith Crowley. And instead of pearls, cashmere sweaters, and skirts, she could now wear baggy shirts and parachute pants. She wasn't even styling her hair anymore, rather letting it fall naturally around her face. More importantly, she was gaining confidence writing for the newspaper—and had a great relationship with Dash.

Dash grabbed his leather jacket from the back of his chair and stuck a pencil behind his ear. "Ready to rock? Ready to go over to Greek Row and make those frat beasts run for cover?"

"Ready," Lauren assured him, with a little more confidence than she really felt. Just thinking about fraternity row made Lauren nervous.

Dash quickly kissed her mouth. "Let's hit it."

Lauren grabbed her notepad and led the way to the door. "I still can't believe those ODT frat guys never did their community service," she told Dash as they left the noisy basement newspaper office and trotted up the stairs.

"I can."

"But we caught them red-handed," Lauren went on. They avoided a Frisbee game just outside the door and detoured onto a bike path. "They made that pledge get drunk last fall, threw him in a car trunk and threatened to make him walk up and down Greek Row without any clothes on. If we hadn't rescued him, who knows what would have happened."

"I know." Dash led the way past the library.

"We exposed them in the newspaper," Lauren said. "They were convicted of hazing by the interfrat council and assigned twenty hours of community service."

"Lauren, how many times are you going to go over this?"

"As many times as I need to," Lauren answered. "Unlike you, I wasn't born with nerves of steel."

"And a noble soul," Dash joked.

"But they never did one minute of community service. Now it's spring rush and they're recruiting new members and telling the potential pledges how great they are. It makes me sick."

Dash stopped in front of her and grinned. "That's the spirit. That's just what I want you to say when we get over to the ODT house and you have to face Christopher Hammond."

Lauren gulped. Her stomach clenched and she couldn't speak as they hurried past the athletic fields and headed off campus to fraternity row. She thought about Christopher Hammond. He would be harder to face than the rest of his fraternity combined. Handsome and crafty, Christopher was a bigwig with the ODTs. Worse, he'd tried to stop the hazing article from being published by charming Lauren into thinking he was innocent. Lauren had even let him kiss her because she hadn't known how to stop him, and that had almost ruined things with Dash. That's why Lauren was so nervous—she knew this was a test. If she could face Christopher Hammond again and be tough, she could prove to Dash that the old, scared, society Lauren was gone forever. Most importantly, she could prove it to herself.

They reached the last stoplight before turning onto frat row. Dash stopped and smiled at her. "You okay?"

"Sure. Why shouldn't I be?"

"You haven't said anything for a while."

"You know me." Lauren tried to laugh, as some fraternity pledges in suits and ties strutted by. "I'm the strong, silent type."

The light turned green, but Lauren couldn't get her feet to move.

"Lauren, you're not wimping out on me, are you?" Dash asked.

"No. Never." Lauren put a hand to her soft middle. "The word wimp is not even in my vocabulary," she bluffed.

"And we all know, you have a great vocabulary," Dash teased in a Groucho voice. He put his arm around her and led the way to the ODT house.

The rush crowd attending the open house was pressed up against the mismatched furniture of the main reception room. Dash and Lauren squeezed in.

"I feel like we landed on the planet of the preppies," Dash whispered in Lauren's ear.

Lauren nodded as she looked around at the eager, male crowd. Most of the guys looked like freshmen, and were dressed in sportcoats or pressed shirts and ties. They were all chatting and laughing until a hush came over the room. Lauren saw that Christopher was making his way down from the second floor. He acted like he was running for state senator, smiling his winning smile and shaking every hand en route to the front of the room.

"Man, if that smile got any oilier, we could use his face as engine grease," quipped Dash.

Every muscle in Lauren's body was getting tense.

Christopher reached the front of the room and held up his hands. He was tall, with blond hair and a square-jawed face that was born for prime-time television. He actually wanted to work in TV and was an intern for the local news station. His loosened tie, tan slacks, and crisp, white shirt gave him an air of casual authority. Everyone applauded, then fell into awed silence.

"Welcome," Christopher said. "Sorry it's so crowded, but we can't help it if we're the most popular house on the row. You can't argue with success."

"I can," Lauren grumbled.

Dash squeezed her shoulder.

Christopher's charm and confidence carried to every corner of the crowded room. "This fraternity boasts the highest standards of any at the University of Springfield. We have strict academic requirements. Most of our brothers are involved in sports, debate, the international club, the performing arts, and any number of other important activities on campus. Also, our commitment to charity work is strong."

"Maybe they figure hauling beer kegs into ODT qualifies as charity work," Dash whispered to Lauren.

Christopher continued to orate. "For those of you who want to be doing something meaningful during your college years, you should know that last year ODT raised $4,000 for Students Against Drunk Drivers."

The audience applauded, obviously impressed.

"How about Students for Hazing," whispered Dash. "How much money did they raise for that?"

"I think I'm going to throw up," said Lauren.

Christopher waited for the applause to die down. "Some of the most influential people in the United States have been members of this fraternity. Our donations are high, so we have a good budget for activities. He paused for effect. "That means we can afford to have fun."

The audience applauded appreciatively.

"Anybody have any questions?" Christopher asked with a big smile.

"The time is now," Dash urged.

Lauren froze.

Dash waited for her to take the floor. When she didn't, he raised his hand. Christopher looked over with his easy smile, until his eyes locked onto Lauren's. He was about to frown, but quickly covered his concern. "Uh, yes?"

"Listen up, Hammond," Dash began. "You, Mark Geisslinger, Paul Schultz, and Matt Brunengo were assigned twenty hours of community service as punishment for a hazing incident last fall. So far, none of you has put in a single hour. I guess that says a lot about your commitment to charity work."

A shocked hush traveled through the group of prospective pledges.

Christopher pursed his lips and shoved his hands in his pockets, but managed to maintain his effortless smile. "I'm afraid you're giving everyone here the wrong impression."

"We don't print wrong impressions in the school paper," Dash countered. "Hazing is illegal, but your fraternity engages in it anyway.

If these guys are going to pledge your house, they should know what they're in for."

By this time the audience was looking around and beginning to get antsy and nervous. There were whispers and worried looks.

Christopher extended his arms as if he were still in control. "Okay. What this so-called reporter says is very interesting, but it doesn't have much to do with our open house. So before he starts throwing around more accusations, I think he and I should talk in private. In the meantime, please start mingling, eating, and drinking. And don't forget our party this weekend. We expect you all to be here and to have an ODT great time."

The mood lightened up again as the guys laughed and began to socialize.

Meanwhile Dash and Lauren followed Christopher back to the kitchen. The three of them glared at each other for a moment.

"What do you two mean by barging in here like this?" Christopher questioned. "This open house is for pledges only. And if you have a beef with me, you should have the guts to talk to me personally, not hang me in public."

"You already had your trial, Hammond," Dash argued. "And the verdict was guilty."

Christopher looked at Lauren and she swallowed hard. Finally she moved in front of Dash. She knew it was up to her now. She couldn't let Dash take over for her again.

"Hi," Christopher said, turning on his warmest smile. "You're looking good."

Lauren blushed. Then she glanced back at Dash's tense face and drew up her courage. "I'm not here to talk about how I look, Christopher."

"Why are you here, then?"

She held her notebook against her chest as though it could protect her, and took a deep breath. "I'm here to talk to you. And you're here to listen. You, Mark, Matt, and Paul owe this school twenty hours of community service. I am volunteering to make sure that you serve it. If you do, I won't bother you anymore. But if you don't, I'll write another article about you and the ODT house that will make the last one look like a wedding announcement."

Christopher's eyes got big. Dash started to smile.

"What do you want us to do?" Christopher

asked, clearly annoyed. "It's the middle of rush. I'm a very busy person."

"I don't care if it's Christmas day," Lauren spat back, amazed at the force in her voice. "Dash and I have it figured out. Remember those elderly people who live on Bickford Lane, just off campus. I gave you a big scoop for the TV station when the university wanted to tear their houses down and build a parking lot. Well, those people have a hard time doing things for themselves. I want you and your three buddies to meet me at Bickford Lane on Friday at exactly four o'clock, and I want you to help those people clean up their homes. They need walls and windows washed, carpets shampooed, and toilets scrubbed."

Christopher's expression darkened. "What?" he blurted out in disbelief.

Lauren started to shrink inside, but she mustered a last bit of courage. At the same time she felt Dash's hand on her shoulder. "You heard me. You'll be doing the work under my supervision. If you don't show up, I promise you a newspaper article that you will never forget."

Christopher's mouth opened in protest, but

Lauren quickly slipped her arm around Dash's waist and reached for the kitchen door.

"Remind me never to get you too mad at me," Dash teased, as he and Lauren walked back toward campus.

Lauren laughed, knocked into him, and kissed his cheek. "I will."

Three

....

"here am I?"

"Hello, Courtney. I'm Dr. Beecher."

"Who?"

"The doctor taking care of you. You're in University Hospital."

"The hospital? What happened?"

"You had an accident. You hit your head on a canoe at Mill Pond, but you're going to be just fine."

Courtney heard the voices but still didn't quite understand. She remembered something about water and canoes, but she also remembered it was the middle of spring rush. Somehow the two things didn't seem to go together.

Courtney turned and tried to sit up. A sharp pain shot through the back of her head. She heard herself groan, but it was like listening to another person. She closed her eyes, and when she opened them again she saw pale green walls, white curtains, and faces looking down at her. There was the smell of iodine and the feel of rough, clean sheets against her skin. A small bandage was stuck just over her eyebrow and her hair was covered with a paper cap.

My God, I'm in the hospital in the middle of rush week! she suddenly realized. Her mouth went dry and she coughed twice before someone passed her a glass of water. Finally she focused on the man who had been talking to her. He had thick glasses, pale skin, and a white coat with a nametag pinned to his breast pocket.

"Courtney, I want you to count backwards starting from ten," Dr. Beecher said.

"Why would I want to do that?"

"Just do it please."

"Ten, nine, eight, seven, six, five, four, three, two, one."

"Very good. You've had a mild concussion," Dr. Beecher said. "We don't think it's serious, but we want you to stay in bed for a while just to be sure. You may experience a little bit of amnesia, but don't let that concern you."

Courtney couldn't believe what she was hearing. Was this doctor telling her that she couldn't get out of bed? That was impossible. She had a million things to do. Her sorority couldn't get along without her, certainly not during rush. This time when she sat up she ignored the pain and looked directly at Dr. Beecher. "I can't stay here," she insisted. "I have to get back to my sorority house."

Dr. Beecher shook his head. "You're under observation. We can't let you go just yet."

"But you don't understand. We're in the middle of choosing new girls. I have to be there."

"We know," a nurse with freckles on her nose said in a soothing voice. "Your sorority friends have been calling the hospital all afternoon."

"They have?"

"Yes, they're all very worried."

"They are?"

"The only thing you have to do is get well, young lady," insisted Dr. Beecher, "and we're here to help you do that. We're going to let you rest now, but push this button if you need someone from the nurses' desk." He showed Courtney a small hand control with a call button. "Just buzz if you need anything," he said, placing the control on the bedstand and going to the door.

The nurse and other doctor bustled out. After they left it was suddenly very quiet. Courtney looked down at herself to see if she was all there. Her slim figure was swathed in a shapeless, green hospital gown. She picked up a small mirror on top of her bedstand. Just as she thought, she looked awful. Someone had left her purse near the mirror, but she didn't bother with makeup. She was too busy thinking about what had happened. She remembered catching her shoe on a plank, and the sound of people screaming.

"KC, Faith, and Winnie," Courtney suddenly said.

They had probably taken her to the hospital. The rushees had been too panicked to react. Besides, they probably hadn't wanted to ruin their beautiful clothes and perfect makeup.

Courtney put the mirror down and trembled. Most of the girls in the Tri Betas were wonderful, but Courtney knew that a few of them were phonies. She had managed to get rid of one of the worst, Marielle Danner, but there would be more Marielles. Courtney wanted friends, not ruthless climbers. She wanted friends who weren't afraid to tease her and cry with her; friends who would support her when she needed help, or jump in a cold pond if she hit her head.

She reached for the slim leather appointment book inside her purse, but was stopped by a quiet knock on her door. "Hello," Courtney called out.

The door opened a crack and two familiar faces appeared in the doorway.

"Courtney," blurted KC. She was carrying a bouquet of daisies. Behind her was Diane.

"Are you okay?" Diane asked in a panicked voice.

"I wish people would quit asking me that," Courtney groused. Seeing Diane just reminded her of everything she had to do. "I'm fine, actually. I'm ready to get out of here."

"Everyone is so worried," Diane insisted, as she hurried over to Courtney and gave her a warm hug.

KC held out the bouquet and Courtney sniffed the flowers appreciatively. "Thanks, KC. I love daisies." She stuck the flowers in her water pitcher.

"Don't you want them in a nice vase, Courtney?" Diane asked.

Courtney shrugged. "I don't care. Now tell me what's been happening since this dumb accident of mine."

Diane looked puzzled. "Are you really sure you don't want a vase? We'd never leave flowers in a plastic water pitcher at the sorority house."

For some reason, Courtney liked the flowers sticking out of her yellow, plastic pitcher. "I'll get a vase from the nurse after you leave," she fibbed, then pulled on her hospital gown and readjusted her pillows.

This seemed to satisfy Diane, who suddenly began talking to Courtney in her most soothing voice. "I just want you to know you don't have to worry about anything. I'll take care of house business until you're well."

"Thanks, Diane, but you can't do it all without me," Courtney said. Her sore head was suddenly filled with details. There were decorations to make, rejection and callback notes to write, parties and interviews to arrange. Courtney suddenly swung back her covers and got to her feet. The floor was freezing; she was wobbly and she felt dizzy. Still, she managed to stagger across the room.

Just then, Dr. Beecher poked his head into the room. Courtney tried to intimidate him with her best sorority president stare, but he wasn't buying it. In fact, he intimidated *her*. "What are you doing?" he asked.

"Nothing."

"Good, that's exactly what you're supposed to be doing—nothing!" He stayed by the door and crossed his arms.

KC looked as concerned as the doctor. She took Courtney's arm and led her back to bed. Courtney felt her spirits sink.

"Don't ever try that again," Dr. Beecher warned. "You could suffer short-term memory loss, even a personality change or seizures. You have to be careful for a while. So no more getting out of bed without permission, understand?"

Courtney nodded sullenly.

"And one more thing. No more visitors today." Dr. Beecher shook his head and let the door swing hard. His footsteps echoed down the hall.

Diane and KC looked at one another.

"I'M GOING TO GO OUT OF MY MIND," Courtney shouted.

"You don't feel well," KC insisted. "You've got to take it easy, Courtney. Just like the doctor said."

"Don't worry," Diane tried to reassure her. "You'll be fine real soon. In the meantime, I'll take care of everything. All the sisters will pitch in to help. We have a great group of girls and a great group of rushees this spring."

"I guess I don't have much choice," Courtney sighed, sinking under the covers again. She hugged KC and Diane one more time, then waved them out. As soon as they were gone, she threw back the covers and tried to get out of bed again. This time no doctor came in, but her head hurt so much she stopped herself. She got back into bed, closed her eyes, and began to cry.

"Oh, Josh."
"Winnie."

"Josh."

"Win."

Winnie closed her eyes for the kiss, and suddenly stumbled on the steps of Rapids Hall. Grabbing the handrail, she realized with horror that she'd been dreaming on her feet. "Snap out of it," she mumbled to herself. "Josh isn't about to kiss you anytime soon."

The two of them had been through a series of ups and downs since they had first met. Winnie loved Josh Gaffey, a computer major who lived down the hall from her in Forest Dorm—and she was sure that Josh loved her, but she wasn't sure that she and Josh were ever going to get together again. Not after the last setback involving Travis Bennett, an old boyfriend of hers. Travis was out of the picture now, but Josh wasn't back in.

"Confused, crazy, and irresistible," Winnie said, managing to smile. "That's still me."

At least Winnie's life was half sane these days, as opposed to the last few weeks when she had been a total wreck. She had been so demented that she had called a crisis hotline. She had even visited the hotline office and had ended up becoming a counselor and volunteer. The idea of helping other people had been a big, important step for her own recovery.

"Counselor Winnie," she joked to herself. "The blind leading the blind. Or the wacko counseling the weird."

Today she was helping spread the word about the hotline service, and Rapids Hall was the last dorm where she had tacked up a Springfield Crisis Hotline flyer on a central bulletin board. Now each student would know that the Crisis Hotline was there to help them. The hotline had certainly helped her get halfway back on track.

"It's amazing how thinking about other peoples' problems makes our own problems seem less intense," she told herself. She jogged across the quad, skirting a volleyball game, then slowed down as she passed the theater and took a shortcut leading off campus. She was headed to the hotline office.

Fifteen minutes later, she was in a bustling business area with brick buildings and small shops. The Crisis Hotline office was in the center of the block—a dim, dull place behind smeary windows where nobody would look twice. A painted sign lit by spotlights read:

"SPRINGFIELD CRISIS HOTLINE: Help When You Need It."

Stepping inside the building, Winnie was assaulted by the sound of ringing phones, the look of chunky desks and finger-stained green walls. Five people sat hunched over their cluttered desks, talking on telephones. The oldest of the three, Teresa Gray, was a psychology grad student. She helped supervise the volunteers, and she hopped up when she finished with her call.

"Hi, Winnie. Ready for today's training session?" Teresa asked.

"Sure am. Ready, willing, and occasionally mentally able," Winnie said. She let her carpetbag drop on the floor with a loud clunk. Although Winnie had begun taking calls from the moment she had walked into the Hotline office, she was still in training. She dragged one of the metal chairs up to a desk and straddled it like a horse.

"Okay, here we go." Teresa pulled a chair alongside her, pushed papers off the messy desk, and began. "Now, I think you know this already, but we'll go over it once more. All conversations must remain confidential—unless a caller threatens violence or discloses something that must be reported to the police."

"Got it," said Winnie. As much as she liked to talk, she hadn't divulged a single detail of any conversation she had had—not even the time Josh called, talking about how much he loved her. Of course, Josh hadn't known that he was speaking to Winnie, and keeping that conversation to herself had almost caused her to explode.

"Counselors use initials rather than their full names to maintain privacy," said Teresa.

Winnie nodded. "I've already been doing that." She shifted position, folding her legs under her. She opened her notebook and began taking notes.

"When life-threatening or difficult problems come up, volunteers are to pass calls on to the more experienced counselors," Teresa reminded her. "Most calls won't be like that, as you know. Now, when you're speaking to a caller, what must you keep foremost in your mind?"

"I have to be supportive of the caller; get them to stop thinking of themselves as a victim; pinpoint the problem, and help the caller be assertive in finding realistic solutions," Winnie recited.

Teresa patted her on the back. "Good for you. You've been doing your homework."

Winnie grinned. "Well, you know, my mom is a therapist, so I grew up on this stuff. I just didn't take any of it too seriously until now."

"The time has come," said Teresa, smiling. "Okay, Winnie, you're on your own."

Winnie arranged herself at the old desk and chose one of the blinking red lights on the phone. "Crisis Hotline . . . may I help you?"

"I-I'm desperate," the caller, a girl, said in a breathy voice.

"Yes. We all feel that way sometimes. Maybe I can help," said Winnie. She tried to mentally shut out the other sounds in the room, the ringing phones, the clacking typewriter, the careful, measured voices of the other hotline volunteers.

"I don't know. I think I'm a pretty hard person to help," the caller said, her voice shaking.

"Well, why don't you begin by telling me some of the things that are going on with you right now," suggested Winnie.

"I don't know where to start. I guess I should tell you my name, but I can't."

"You are assured confidentiality," said Winnie, pleased that she sounded so professional.

"But I can't tell you who I am!"

"Make up a name."

"Just call me Desperate."

"Okay, Desperate."

"I've lost everything I care about," the girl blurted out. "Even my self respect. I can't face anyone. I used to have everyone's admiration, but now. . . ." Tears stopped her words.

"I know how that is," Winnie said.

"You do? Really?"

"Well, sort of. There have been times in my own life when I've felt like I had no self respect, nothing." *And not so long ago, either,* Winnie thought to herself. *I mean, why do you think I walked into this place?* But of course, she kept those crazy thoughts to herself. She had to be careful she didn't turn into a motor mouth when she was answering her calls.

"I had an important position and I lost it. And everything else with it," Desperate went on. "I don't really know who I am now. I really am desperate."

Winnie was quiet for a moment, trying to

figure out if Desperate was really desperate and needed to talk to someone professional.

As if reading her mind, Desperate said, "Look, I just need to have my life back the way it was. I need to know how to do that, do you understand?"

Winnie breathed a sigh of relief. Obviously, the caller was not going to do anything drastic. "Well, Desperate, it sounds like you need a support system. Perhaps you could renew some of your friendships. Stop thinking of yourself as a victim."

"Do I do that?" asked Desperate.

"It sounds like you might be doing that," said Winnie gently. "I hear you saying that all these things have happened to you. You, the victim."

"I never thought of it that way," said Desperate.

"Why not take one practical step toward improving your life—something that will put you back on track again?"

"That's a good idea. I'll think about it. I mean, I'll do it, I really will."

"Good."

"Can I call and talk to you again sometime?"

"Of course, just ask for W.G.," said Winnie.

"It was good to talk to you, W.G. I think you helped me. Thanks."

" 'Bye, Desperate," Winnie pressed the red button and breathed deeply, letting satisfaction sink in.

Winnie wished every call was as easy. She also wished she could apply the advice she gave callers to her own life. She put her chin in her hands and thought about Josh again. When Josh had called, he had talked about how his life hadn't been the same since he and Winnie had split up, how he still loved her. Loved her! But she had to keep that conversation, like all the others, completely confidential. She, Winnie Gottlieb, girl with the A-number one, gigantic motor mouth, could not talk about the single most important thing that had happened in her life to anyone —not even to Faith or KC, who knew her deepest and darkest secrets. And of course she couldn't mention it to Josh.

She had no idea what to do about it, and it was driving her crazy.

Four

·····················

"**C**ourtney, you are going to pay for this," Marielle Danner hissed between gritted teeth. Angrily, she pulled her straight, brown hair behind one ear, and pounded her manicured hand against her new dorm-room wall.

"Hey, lighten up, Marielle. It's not as bad as that," Marielle's boyfriend, Mark Geisslinger, told her. "So you got kicked out of the Tri Betas. You'll live."

"Easy for you to say," Marielle shot back. "You're still living in the ODT fraternity house, while I'm living in this dumpy dorm."

Mark wiped sweat off his brow as he stacked Marielle's heavy boxes in one corner. "I'm still in ODT but now I have to go clean old peoples' houses with Christopher. Tell me which one of us has it worse."

Marielle pouted.

"You've sure got a lot of stuff, Marielle."

"No one can have too much stuff, Mark. It's just that nothing fits in this little hovel."

Marielle wanted to cry. In mid-semester, the only dorm room she'd been able to find was in Langston Hall, the girls-only study dorm—the dorm KC Angeletti lived in. Fortunately, Marielle hadn't run into KC yet. She'd made a point of avoiding her.

"This place is like a monastery. The bed is as hard as a board," complained Marielle loudly. "And just look at the walls!"

The walls were drab, white and pockmarked with thumbtack holes from the previous resident's poster decor. "The only thing that would help this room would be a bulldozer."

Mark slipped his arms around Marielle's thin waist and tried to hold her close, but she stiffened in his arms. "It's been so long since I've seen you," he said, but Marielle wriggled out of his embrace and straightened her short, tight, knit skirt.

"I'm not in the mood, Mark," she told him firmly.

Mark didn't give up easily. He led her over to the bed and pushed aside her designer closet bag. "Well, you were in the mood to finally call me. For a while, I didn't even hear from you. What happened?"

Marielle gave him a flirty look and blew him a kiss. "I had a slight change of heart." Then she angrily kicked one of her boxes. "You know, every time I look at all this stuff, it reminds me of how Courtney kicked me out of the Tri Betas," she said, more to herself than to Mark. "And I have to do something about it."

"Oh, yeah. Like what?" Mark propped himself on his elbows and watched her.

"I don't know yet," she said, pacing from one end of the small room to the other. "Something, though."

The humiliation and pain of being kicked out of Tri Beta still stung Marielle. She woke up every morning replaying the entire scene of Courtney telling her she was expelled. And worse, her sorority sisters had seemed to stop showing interest in her the moment Courtney had dropped the axe. "I just wish something could happen that would make it possible for me to get back in," she finally admitted.

"Like what?"

"Like Courtney being removed from the presidency."

"That'll never happen. She's Ms. Perfect, isn't she?" Mark said.

Marielle shook her head. "I don't know. I'll wait and see what happens. If she makes one wrong move, I'll be there to jump on her. I would love to see her highness dethroned. But most of all . . ." Marielle's voice became low, as she finally crawled up next to Mark and wrapped her arms around him. "I want to make her the victim."

"Hello."

Courtney thought she was dreaming. The voice was soft and rich.

"Hello?" it repeated again.

Hello, Courtney answered in her dream. *I'm here. Please take me out of this hospital. Please take me away from my life. I knew I was ready for a change before this happened. A tiny part of me was ready to kick up my heels and find something new.*

But being in the hospital was not the kind of change I had in mind.

"Hope I'm not disturbing you."

Oh, that's okay. You're only a dream after all. So disturb me all you want. Let's dance in the middle of my hospital room. I won't worry what other people think. Let me forget who I'm supposed to be for a few hours and we'll laugh and laugh until we can't laugh any more.

"But I have to sit here with you and make sure. . . ."

Sit here with me? How nice. I'd love to listen to your warm, sweet voice and . . . hey, this isn't a dream!

Courtney shot up from under the covers, and with eyes wide open, stared at the young man standing at the foot of her bed. She didn't know when he'd come in, but he had dark, brown eyes and long hair pulled back in a ponytail. He wore a green scrub shirt tucked into jeans with a beaded cowboy belt. An old watch hung from one of his belt loops and a tiny, carved bird dangled from a leather thong around his neck.

"Hello," he said again. His voice was soft and warm.

"Oh. Hi." Courtney pulled up the blankets

close to her throat. She blushed. This guy didn't look old enough to be a medical student and he wasn't carrying a chart.

He gave her an easy smile, and without any more discussion, flopped his lanky body into her bedside chair and pulled out a paperback book of poetry.

Courtney was suddenly sure that she was dreaming again. She sat up and stared.

He just kept reading, different expressions floating over his handsome, boyish face. The longer he sat there, the more Courtney wanted to fling the book out of his hand and throw it at him. She was still disoriented, but she was starting to want to know just exactly what was going on.

Without looking up from his book, he pointed at the bedstand. "I brought the vase," he said.

"What?"

"Your friend said you needed a vase." He shrugged, and met her eyes. "There it is."

"I don't need a . . ." Courtney looked over at KC's flowers, still stuck in her plastic water pitcher, and it all came back to her: Diane, rush, Mill Pond, KC, all the girls that were depending on her at the Tri Beta house. Without thinking, she threw her covers back.

The young man stuck his poetry book back in his pocket. "What are you doing?"

"What am I doing?" Courtney railed, grabbing for a bathrobe. "That's some question for you to be asking me." She remembered that she was wearing a gown that only had ties in the back, and that since she'd been been brought to the hospital directly from Mill Pond, she had no bathrobe. All she saw was an old parka with grass stains that must belong to whoever he was that was sitting next to her bed, reading poetry. Undaunted, she grabbed his parka, swung her legs off the bed, and landed on the floor.

He instantly jumped up and faced her. He was lean and muscular and put his hands out as if he were going to wrestle her.

"Who are you!" Courtney demanded. "Get out of my room!"

"Get back into bed first," he said firmly. "And give me back my parka!"

"Just get out of my way. I have a lot of important things to do!"

"No you don't," he argued.

"How do you know? You're some nut who walked in here from I don't know where."

He stuck out his arms and grabbed her shoulders.

"Don't touch me!" Courtney screamed, feeling more and more desperate. She tried to twist around and started getting light-headed again, but he locked his arms around her and held her tight against his chest. She could feel his heart beating.

"I have to touch you," he reasoned. "You're not cooperating."

"I'm going to scream for help," Courtney threatened. "I have to get out of here and make paper streamers for a very important party. I have to cut out one hundred paper picture frames. I'm the president of the Tri Beta sorority and a lot of people are depending on me!"

The boy finally let her wriggle away from him and held her at arm's length. "Gee," he marveled, staring right into her eyes. "You're crazy."

"You're the crazy person. Go back to your ward."

"I'm not from a ward," he said, starting to crack a smile.

"Then where are you from?" Tears were building up in her eyes. "Who are you and why won't you let me go back to my sorority house?"

Suddenly he scooped her up in his arms and before Courtney could take another breath, laid her gently back on the bed. When she was completely tucked in, he leaned over her.

"My name is Phoenix Cates," he said. "I'm a freshman at U. of S. I'm also your orderly. My job is to make sure you stay in bed, and I'm not going to let you out of my sight." He took out his poetry book again.

Courtney pounded the mattress and screamed, but in a few seconds she had fallen back against the bed and drifted off to sleep.

Five

．．．．．．．．．．．．．．．．．

"**D**id you hear about Courtney?"
"She's getting out of the hospital but she'll have to stay in bed."
"I'm worried about her."
"Me, too."
KC snipped carefully at the thick, glossy paper. She was sitting on one of the long, overstuffed living room sofas of Tri Beta house, with three other rushees who were working on picture frames. She tried not to show that she was more worried than the rest of them. It was a privilege having a friendship with Courtney—not just because it would get her into

the sorority easily —but because Courtney was a special person. Now that Courtney's health was in jeopardy, though, KC was worried that her acceptance to Tri Beta might be in jeopardy, too.

"I'm done with these picture frames," KC told Diane.

The small, paper picture frames would eventually frame the baby photos of each rushee and Tri Beta sister. Diane was to draw the photos out of a hat —one hat for rushees, one for members—then match the photos with the girls. After that, they would pair up for interviews. It was another rush tradition.

The preparations were going smoothly, until a moment later when a trio of sisters burst in the front door.

"Oh, no! I forgot about the baby photo interviews!" gasped one harried-looking sister.

"I have an old negative," said another, "but I don't have a print."

"How long does it take to get prints made?" the third fretted.

KC realized that with all the commotion over Courtney, she had forgotten about her photo, too. She had a sudden idea—one that made her stomach jolt—but the situation was serious, and, she didn't want Courtney to have to worry about anything.

KC put down her scissors and walked over to Diane, who was trying to juggle each girl's problem and two rolls of velvet ribbon at the same time.

"Even though I'm just a rushee, would it be all right for me to help?" KC asked.

Diane turned around. "Oh, KC, thank you. Without Courtney we need all the help we can get. But what can you do?"

KC swallowed hard. "I've got a . . . friend who's a photographer. He has a darkroom in his dorm, and he just might be able to get prints made really fast. If I can get everybody's negatives, I bet I can get the pictures done."

Diane sighed with relief. "KC, you're a lifesaver."

Half an hour later, armed with a manila envelope full of old negatives, KC strode across the sunny campus and into Coleridge Hall. She was looking for Peter Dvorsky, a photography major who had taken pictures of her for a U. of S. calendar. She had once asked him to a dance, then dumped him when someone better looking had come along. She had regretted it ever since, and had even made an apology of sorts. But Peter continued to treat her with coolness and infuriating distance.

Someone was singing scales in one of the upstairs dorm rooms, and someone else was playing the trumpet. KC carefully maneuvered her way around an easel set up in the middle of the hall.

Finally, she knocked on the door of Peter's room. No answer.

"Looking for Peter?" asked another guy. "Check the darkroom downstairs."

"Thanks." KC made her way down to the basement, breathing in the smell of paste and acrylic paints.

A large KEEP OUT sign hung on a door with a red-felt penned message underneath: DARKROOM IN USE. KC knocked tentatively.

Peter yanked open the door. He looked at her blankly, as if she were just another in the long line of distractions he'd had that day. KC stared at him with a mixture of confusion and surprise, taken off guard by the sight of his tousled, blond hair and carefree posture. He was wearing an old football jersey and cutoffs and his feet were bare.

Suddenly his expression changed and he

gave her a lopsided grin. "Oh, hey, KC. This is a surprise."

"Uh, am I interrupting something, like maybe a genius at work?" she quipped.

"Naw. I'm just making a few contact sheets." He shoved his hands in his pockets nonchalantly. "What brings you here?"

KC opened the manila envelope with fingers that suddenly felt like all thumbs. "I have a photography problem. See, I have all these negatives of baby pictures and I need them developed right away."

"Baby pictures? Sounds criminal."

"Peter!"

"Okay. Come on in," Peter said, motioning her with a nod of his head.

Tentatively, KC followed him inside. The tiny room was bathed in an amber light, but KC could make out a sign on the wall that read WET ZONE. Beside it, negatives hung from plastic clips on a clothesline. Below was a sink and several trays, filled with strong-smelling solutions. A couple of enlarging machines occupied the corners. The smell of chemicals made KC cough.

Peter apologized. "I know the fumes are bad, but you kinda get used to them after a while." KC nodded, beginning to breathe a little easier. Then she showed him the negatives. Peter held one up to the light. "Pretty important stuff, I see. Mind telling me what this is for?"

"The Tri Betas." KC waited for him to make fun of her sorority ambitions. "It's part of their rush interview."

"Hmmm. This is you, huh? Cute, with a little bit of drool on the chin. *Au naturel.*"

"Very funny."

"Nice shot. Who took it?"

"My dad, probably," she said.

"I wonder how many kids get their pictures taken wearing tie-dyed dresses." He gave her a long look.

KC stared back, wondering what Peter would really think if he ever met her hippie parents. "Peter, just print the pictures. Okay?"

"Okay. Ever been in a darkroom before?" he asked, leaning casually against the counter.

KC's knee bumped him. "Oh sorry."

"No problem." He smiled.

"No, I haven't been in a darkroom," she said. "Why do you ask?"

Peter grinned, shifting his position so that his shoulder brushed hers. "Just wondering."

"Wondering what!"

"Just wondering if this was an excuse to get me in the dark."

KC's face flushed. His remark put her totally off balance, something that didn't happen to her very often. "You wish! Look, if you don't want to do this for me, I can get someone else to."

Peter raised one eyebrow. "Really? That's great. I didn't know you knew a lot of photographers."

"Well, I don't, it's just . . ." KC stammered, heat rising on her cheeks. She was famous for keeping cool when the thermometer rose, but Peter could be so infuriating.

Their eyes met and locked. KC had this odd sensation that Peter could see all the way through her. At the same time she couldn't understand why Peter intrigued her so much. She usually didn't think about guys at all, and Peter was too down-to-earth for a Tri Beta pledge-to-be to show interest in him. Still, KC shivered involuntarily when her bare arm touched his.

"We're only set up for black and white in here," Peter warned, taking the negatives from her.

"That's fine."

"Then here goes. First we put the negative in the enlarger like this." Peter turned out the amber light, then turned on the safelight, a small, glowing, red bulb which would not expose the printing paper.

"Next the paper goes in this tray of chemicals, until the picture appears."

KC watched until she could see her baby picture magically appear on the paper a little at a time. "Wow," she said, as Peter leaned closer for a better look. His hair brushed her cheek and her arm pressed against his.

He used a pair of bamboo tongs to take the photo out of one solution and put it into the next. "This is the stop bath. And now it goes into the fixer. After that, you put the photo in the sink tray and run water over it."

Peter shook water off the photo and hung it up to dry, leaning right in front of KC. Then he turned toward her again and reached up. KC froze. He was going to kiss her. Her heart sped up and her breath stopped. But then he reached past her, taking a towel off an overhead shelf to dry his hands. KC almost collapsed from disappointment. Suddenly Peter switched on a bare, overhead bulb, and put clothespins on the bottom of the print. "There. Voila, as they say."

KC felt let down. "Thanks. Maybe I should come back later when you've done them all."

Peter shrugged. But before KC could open the door, he said, "By the way, there's a dorm party this Friday night. It's sponsored by Rapids Hall. Should be a good time."

KC focused on his thick blond hair, his frayed sleeve and inexpensive watch. She felt a catch in her heart and waited. Was he going to ask her out? Was he finally going to admit that he was impressed by her after all? "Really?" she said.

"Yup. You know those outdoor types get real basic when they throw a party. They usually pull out all the stops. I think they had a rapelling contest up in the mountains last weekend. I can't wait to hear about it."

KC was getting angry. He obviously wasn't going to ask her out. "Well, I can't go to that party because I have to attend an ODT frat party for rush." She waited tensely for his reaction.

"Another gala Geek Row event. Have a good time." He went back to his printing.

KC was ready to climb the darkroom walls.

Here she was, beautiful, intelligent, sought after by the most sought after, and Peter treated her like a drudge.

"Peter," she said, deciding that she would leave before she dumped a tray of fixer on his head. "I'm going to go. I'll be back later to pick up the photos. Do you have anything else to say to me?"

He turned and gave her a huge smile. "Actually, KC, I do."

KC held her breath. At last. "Well?"

"You're welcome," he quipped, going back to his printing. "I'm glad I could help you out."

KC opened the door and slammed it shut behind her.

"I refuse."

"You can't refuse."

"What do you mean I can't refuse. Let me talk to the person in charge!"

"Courtney, I *am* the person in charge."

"That's impossible. You can't be. You look like you should live in a teepee in the woods. And I won't sit in that wheelchair. I can walk."

Phoenix smiled. "It's hospital policy, Courtney. Even though you've only been here for one day and you're pretty much okay now, you have to leave the hospital in a wheelchair. I don't make the rules."

Courtney wanted to scream. Even leaving the hospital was proving to be an ordeal. She couldn't believe that they had assigned Phoenix to her for yet another day. Since eleven that morning he'd been sitting in her room, watching her every move.

Phoenix set the brake on the wheelchair. "Have a seat," he said, as he reached out and started to help Courtney off the bed.

Courtney felt herself lean toward his hands, but then she stiffened. "I can at least get into a wheelchair by myself."

Phoenix moved back.

KC had stopped by that morning with Courtney's clothes and toiletries, so Courtney was starting to feel like the her old self again. She was dressed in a flannel jumper and lace trimmed T-shirt, and her hair was freshly washed. As she sat in the wheelchair and folded her hands, she wondered if Phoenix had noticed that she looked a lot better than she had in her hospital cap and gown. Then she wondered why she even cared.

Phoenix took a blanket from her bed and placed it over her lap. He handed over her possessions, which the hospital had collected in a plastic bag. Her clothes still smelled of pond water.

"I thought you might also want this," he said, pulling a book out of the back pocket of his jeans.

"What is it?"

Phoenix showed her the cover. The book was entitled "Great Rock Poetry," and it looked like it had been read a thousand times. "It's all the best rock lyrics from the last twenty years," he told her.

"Why would I want to read that?"

"I read you some of it today while you were napping after lunch," he answered simply, his brown eyes not showing a hint of defensiveness. "You liked it."

"I did?"

"Well, you were sleeping," Phoenix said, brushing back his hair. "But you were smiling in your sleep."

Courtney didn't know whether to thank him or slug him. The idea of him sitting next to her while she slept was disarming. There was an intimacy about it that made her feel like unfolding the blanket he'd set on her lap and pulling it over her head. "Who are you!" she suddenly blurted, even though she remembered asking him that before. He was Phoenix Cates, orderly, U. of S. freshman, but she still thought he looked too wild to be in college and she still had the sense that he had dropped down from the moon. Even his name sounded made up.

He knelt in front of her to adjust something on the base of the wheelchair. "I told you. I'm an orderly—"

"I know all that," she snapped. "But who are you really? Why did you read to me while I was asleep?"

He looked up at her with his clear eyes.

Courtney couldn't quite believe she was asking such personal questions. After all, it wasn't polite, and he certainly wasn't the kind of guy a sorority president was supposed to want to know more about. But maybe something had changed inside her over the last day, because for the first time in her life, all the polite rules that her parents had instilled in her were blurring into mush.

Phoenix glanced up and smiled. "I read to you because I believe in the power of the unconscious," he said. Then he laughed at himself. "I figured if I read you beautiful poems, the words would go somewhere in your brain and affect your body, and make you well."

Courtney stared.

"I believe in the power of the mind, and the power of nature," he went on. "That's why I'm living in Rapids Hall. They're into all kinds of outdoor trips and stuff having to do with the mountains around here. We're even having a big party this Friday night. That's the nature part, and my classes and reading and stuff are food for the mind."

Courtney tried to follow him.

"I would never have taken a job that wasn't outside in the open air, except that this was the only job I could find and I needed the money. So I read rock poetry while I work and then my mind can take a journey, even if my body can't. I think you have to find ways to live within the rules that life sets for you, but still explore the things that are important to you."

Courtney's mouth had fallen open. For some reason his words echoed down to the core of her proper, well-disciplined self. "How old are you?" she asked bluntly, aware again that she was breaking well-ingrained social rules.

"Eighteen."

That was two years younger than Courtney.

Phoenix smiled and Courtney smiled too. They looked at one another for a long time. Then suddenly aware that at least ten minutes had gone by, Courtney broke the intimate silence. "My friend Diane Woo is picking me up," she said, quietly. "She's probably waiting outside. We'd better go."

Phoenix gave her knee a gentle pat, then walked around behind her and began to push the wheelchair. "Okay. Let's go."

She rolled out of her room and down the hall, past the nurses' station and a series of closed doors. It all smelled of disinfectant until they got to the carpeted lobby, which was scented by flowers and floor wax.

"Hey, I'll recite you a poem as a goodbye," Phoenix finally said as they passed the gift shop and the information desk.

For some reason, the word goodbye created a pang of sadness in Courtney's chest.

"Something about rolling and traveling, and setting yourself free," Phoenix went on. "I mean if Chuck Berry ever had to be carted out of here in a wheelchair, I bet he'd like one of his poems recited back to him."

"Who's Chuck Berry?" Courtney asked. They rolled past the coffee shop toward the bright, sun-filled foyer.

Phoenix did a sharp turn with her chair. "Chuck Berry is a terrific poet and musician."

He pushed the front door open and wheeled her out. But they both went silent when they saw Diane waiting in the loading area, next to a shiny sedan. As soon as Diane saw Courtney she ran over.

"Oh well," Phoenix said, shrugging and coming around to help Courtney up. "Your ride's here. I guess I'll have to save Chuck Berry for another time."

"That's too bad," Courtney said. She stood up on wobbly legs.

"What's too bad?" asked Diane, as she took Courtney's bag.

Courtney and Phoenix looked at one another, savoring their secret and not sharing it with Diane. They both smiled.

"It's nothing," Courtney answered sweetly. Diane went to the car and got back in behind the wheel. "Another time," Courtney repeated to Phoenix, even though she knew there would never be another time. She stuck out her hand for him to shake.

Phoenix took her hand but he didn't shake it. He just held it. "Don't wear yourself out with all those picture frames, or doilies, or whatever it is you have to do," he said, looking deep into Courtney's eyes.

"I won't."

"Maybe I'll see you around sometime."

Courtney laughed. She hardly imagined herself hanging around Rapids Hall, and she couldn't exactly see Phoenix striding up and down Greek Row.

Phoenix held up a warning finger and laughed. "You know Courtney, you should skip the Bandaids."

"What?" Instinctively she reached up and touched the place where the bandage had been on her head.

His eyes hadn't left her face. "You're even more beautiful when you're not wearing hospital green."

"I am?" Courtney blushed. She felt more disoriented now then when she had woken up after the accident.

"Hey, maybe I'll write a poem about you."

"You will?"

Diane honked once and Courtney jumped as if she'd heard a gun shot. She looked toward the car and remembered rush, the Tri Betas, the rest of her high society life. "Goodbye."

"Goodbye," Phoenix echoed.

Their hands touched, but Courtney couldn't look at him. She didn't know why, but she was fighting off tears again.

Six

Clackety clackety clack clack. . . .
The sound of tap-dancing feet
rapped out a rhythm overhead as
Winnie and Faith scurried through the lobby,
away from Faith's dorm.

Winnie lugged her carpetbag, which was
loaded down with books and cassette tapes of
the lectures she and Faith had missed for Western Civ. "It's like that guy is tap dancing on
our heads," Winnie joked, doing a tap dance
of her own in her bright, pink Unitard and
lime green sweater vest. "Maybe we should
have stayed here after all and turned our lec-

ture tapes up to full volume, just to get revenge."

"Could you listen to Professor Hermann's lecture at full volume?" Faith asked.

"No," they both said at the same time as they trotted out onto the green. They had planned to study in Faith's room, but had vacated, not because of the tap dancer, but because of Lauren. She was a creative writing major, and was working on a "write to music" assignment—one where she had to use a piece of music to get deeper into her writing.

"I still can't believe what Lauren just told us about having to make those frat guys clean houses," Winnie marveled. "I think she should write to music about that."

Faith shook her head. "She'd need grand opera for those jerks." Faith had once dated Christopher Hammond and had no illusions of him being a great guy.

"Forget them. Let's go to my room," Winnie suggested as they crossed the grass. She stepped over a girl who'd fallen asleep with a book over her face.

"Your dorm is always so crazy," Faith said, pushing her long braid over her shoulder. "How will we hear the lecture tapes?"

"True, they don't call my place Party Dorm for nothing," Winnie babbled. "But where else can we go? We have to make up the lectures we missed or Hermann will send us to Western Civ jail or something. And I'm spending a fair amount of my study time at the hotline now, so I can't get any further behind." Winnie climbed a bench and jumped down. "And then there's all the rest of the time I waste thinking about Josh."

"Why don't you just tell Josh you love him, Winnie? Tackle him in the hall and blurt out the words."

"Faith!" Winnie pretended to be shocked. Then she nudged her friend. "You're right. I should take charge of my destiny, like I tell all those people who call the hotline to do. Hey. Speaking of advice, I've got to tell you about one of my callers."

"I thought you weren't supposed to talk about them."

"It's okay as long as I don't mention any names," Winnie said. "This one was really in dump city. The first time she called I told her not to be such a victim, and she called again just last night and asked for me. Can you believe it? She said she took my advice and was doing a lot better."

"Oh, Winnie, that's wonderful. I bet that makes you feel good."

"It does. I never thought I did anything very important before. Not only was I an undeclared major, I was an undeclared human."

They walked into Forest Hall, which as usual was pretty rowdy. A foursome was doing the limbo in the lobby and a stereo was booming upstairs. Winnie swung into the rhythm as she and Faith walked down her hallway. Popcorn flew out an open door, landing in Winnie's spiked hair. She plucked it out as she passed Josh's room. The door was closed.

"You know," Winnie told Faith in a quiet voice, "every time I pass his room, I think maybe, just maybe, I'll see him."

Faith gave her a sympathetic look.

Winnie reached her own door, hesitated for a second, then fished out her key. "Home sweet home." But when she opened the door, she groaned. At the same time, Faith stared into the room, gasped, and turned away.

Winnie's roommate, track star and study grind, Melissa McDormand, and Faith's former high school sweetheart, Brooks Baldwin, were lying on the floor, with their limbs entwined. Mel's sweatshirt was up over her ribcage, and Brooks's arm was draped over her shoulder. Both of them were completely unaware that either Winnie or Faith were standing there.

This is happening much too often lately, Winnie thought, anger boiling up inside her. Since Melissa and Brooks had fallen for one another, they seemed to have forgotten that other people in the world existed. Lately, Winnie was always walking in on them when they were in a hot and heavy embrace.

Soundlessly, Winnie and Faith backed up and shut the door behind them. Faith's face was beet red.

"I'm really sorry," Winnie said. "My room was a dumb idea."

"Tri Beta, Tri Beta, the finest and the true . . ."

A group of rushees linked arms on the front lawn of the Tri Beta house, singing a rush song they had set to a popular tune. Other girls scurried around in high gear carrying blue and white crêpe paper streamers and baskets of fresh flowers.

"Hurry up—I've got English Lit in five minutes."

"Oh, no! That reminds me—I've got a language lab today. How are we supposed to do all this stuff?"

"Rush means what it says: rushing around."

The noise added to KC's excitement as she sat on the Tri Beta porch, chatting with Leona Fieldston, an active sister. "So I've been looking forward to being a member of Tri Beta ever since I came to U. of S. I rushed in the fall," KC reminded her, "but it didn't work out." She knew Leona was aware that she had dropped out of rush after insulting Marielle Danner as revenge for the cruel way Marielle had treated Lauren.

Leona smiled. "I'm glad you feel that way, KC. Courtney has always spoken well of you. I'm sure everything will go smoothly this time."

"How is Courtney?" KC asked.

Leona shrugged. "She's back, but she's on bedrest. No one has seen her except Diane."

Before Leona could say anything else, they were interrupted by a petite, red-haired rushee who appeared in the doorway. "KC Angeletti?" she asked, nervously.

"Yes?"

The rushee fidgeted. "Um, Courtney would like to see you upstairs. Diane told me to tell you."

KC smiled, first at the rushee, then at Leona. "Thank you. Well, it was good talking to you, Leona."

"Same here." Leona shook her hand warmly.

KC rushed into the Tri Beta house and hurried up the staircase, past the antique telephone, the posters, and little chairs placed decoratively in the hall. She knocked gently on Courtney's door.

"Come in," said Courtney.

KC opened the door. Courtney was sitting up in bed with masses of lace pillows stacked behind her lovely, blond head. She looked peaceful, wearing an unlikely flannel nightgown. Some study notes were scattered across the blue bedspread. KC looked around the small room and saw family photos, ski posters, and a computer and mini stereo on the desk.

Diane was at the bedside, her head bent over papers. She barely looked up when KC entered. "Courtney, we have so much to do," Diane said, shaking her head. She held up first one list, then another. "We have to do all the decorating for the ODT party, and then there are the final rush interviews to finish up."

"Hi, KC," said Courtney, motioning KC to a blue chair on the other side of her bed.

"How are you?" KC asked.

Courtney gave her a funny, almost mischievous smile.

"Courtney," Diane went on. "I'm sorry to have to make you deal with all this, but I need to know what you think of Delia Bunter and Margaret Kaplan." Diane glanced at KC. "Cover your ears, KC. Don't you dare repeat a word of this."

"KC can listen," Courtney replied. "They're both very nice girls, I guess."

Diane looked puzzled. "Okay. What about Sheila Wyatt and Bernadette Wing?"

"I don't want to decide the fate of those girls right now, Diane," Courtney objected. "I've been away. I can barely remember who they are."

"But we have to decide which girls to call back for final interviews!" Diane insisted.

"Call them all back," Courtney said gaily.

Diane slapped her lists down on her lap. "Courtney! We also have to figure out what decorations to bring over to the ODT party on Friday night."

Courtney shrugged.

"And we need to arrange the Saturday visit to the Springfield Children's Clinic. We should have all the girls tour the ward, since it's our house's charity."

Courtney clapped her hands to her face. "Do we have to!" she cried. "I don't think those kids like it when we come through their hospital in such big groups."

Diane looked stunned. "Courtney, you're usually so together about this."

"Yes, I know." Courtney looked at KC, then threw up her hands. "I'm just not feeling very well right now. Would you mind leaving me alone with KC for a moment?"

Diane looked from Courtney to KC and back again. Finally, she shook her head, collected her notes, and left.

Courtney looked right at KC. She wasn't sure whether to burst into tears or wild laughter. It felt as if everything in her life was topsy-turvy. She didn't know if it was because of the bump on the head, or Phoenix, or that feeling that something extraordinary was going to happen. But whatever it was, she was simply unable to react in the old, rigid way. She laughed nervously. "I guess I've had a lot of time to think about things since I hit my head, KC. Suddenly all the details of rush are beginning to seem sort of silly. Isn't that weird?"

KC stared.

"I mean I still love my sorority and I want to see the best girls get into Tri Beta," Courtney explained. "But I keep thinking about other things, like this rock song I was listening to all morning."

"A rock song?" KC questioned.

Courtney shook her head. "I don't know. I mean, I've been thinking about the all-important ODT party on Friday night. Diane told me that Christopher Hammond and Mark Geisslinger have some twisted prank planned, and I'm not sure I want to be there to see it."

KC was speechless. Last fall Lauren had been led to believe that she was Christopher Hammond's dream date, only to find out that it was a nasty joke. Remembering how both she and Courtney had stood by and watched Lauren be humiliated still made KC feel sick.

"What can you do?" KC asked. "That kind of thing is part of rush."

"But why do I have to go along with it?" Courtney sighed. She put her hands to her face. "Maybe this is just what the doctors warned me about. What was it? Memory loss? Personality change?"

KC nodded. "I have to confess that as much as I've wanted to be a Tri Beta, there've been a few times during rush when I wished I could have had memory loss."

Courtney got a dreamy expression. "Just this once, I'd like to skip the ODT party and do something crazy."

"You?"

Courtney looked right at her. "Yes, me."

KC's shock was all over her perfect face. Then she bit her lip and looked away. "You know, if you really wanted to skip the ODT party, and if you were well enough . . . forget it, you won't want to do this."

"What?" Courtney pushed. "KC. What!"

KC shifted. "There's a dorm party this Friday night. I'm sure you wouldn't want to go. It's being given by Rapids Hall, where all these nature types live."

"Rapids Hall?" Courtney cried, sitting so

far forward she almost fell off her bed. "Really?"

"Really," KC said. "But I'm sure you don't want to go. I shouldn't have mentioned it. Besides, you'll probably still be in bed."

Courtney smiled broadly. "The doctor said I could do whatever I wanted, starting tomorrow. And I want to go to that party. KC, I'll skip the ODT party and go to the dorm party if you will."

KC stared at her in amazement. "Courtney, I'm just a rushee. I can't skip a required frat party."

Courtney grinned. "If you're with me, you can."

"Courtney, I don't understand," KC mumbled. "What's going on?"

Courtney flung her head back against her pillows in a sudden, joyful movement. "KC, ever since rush began I've been feeling like something amazing was going to happen. But it won't happen if I just stay in my room, or on Greek Row. For once in my ordered life, I want to do something wild. I want to take a chance." She paused and smiled again. "Rapids Hall party, here we come."

Seven

....

A slight wind lifted Lauren's wispy hair and rattled the loose windows of the old houses on Bickford Lane. A bonfire burned somewhere, sending big, black flakes into the air, but Lauren barely noticed. Her insides already felt like she had swallowed ash.

"I see maid service has arrived, and not a minute too soon," Mark Geisslinger said, pointing at Lauren and grinning at Paul Schultz and Matt Brunengo.

"Hey, guys, I thought we ordered a sexy French maid, not a dog," Matt spouted.

"What a yuck."

"What a zero on a scale of one to ten."

Christopher didn't say anything. He merely glared at Lauren from across the porch.

Lauren tried to stay calm. She wanted to run away from the frat guys and the dirty, old houses, but she forced herself to act as though she hadn't heard their cruel words. It was the only way she was going to get through the afternoon, and Lauren was determined to see ODT punished for their hazing. Still, it was going to take every ounce of willpower Lauren had. "Mark," Lauren barked, in her toughest voice.

"What? Laaaaaaaurennnnn." Mark answered.

"You're here to work."

Christopher snapped his fingers. He didn't like what Lauren had forced on the fraternity, but he wanted to get it over with as quickly as possible. At Christopher's command, Mark and the two other ODT brothers assembled on the steps of the first rundown house. They laughed when Mark did a little dance around the rickety porch.

"Look," Lauren insisted, ignoring the ridiculous display. "Will you and somebody else carry the cart of cleaning supplies up the stairs, please?"

The cart was loaded down with a vacuum cleaner, mops, brooms, pails, and cleansers, which Lauren had borrowed from her maid's job at the Springfield Mountain Inn. Muscle would be necessary to transport the cart up the stairs, but Mark was acting like the only muscle he had was between his ears. Lauren stared all four guys down, and finally Christopher and Paul picked up the ends of the cart.

"Good," Lauren said. She turned around and went up the stairs herself. At the top she knocked on a door. An old woman wearing glasses, a floral-print dress, and clunky shoes opened the door.

"Mrs. Redding?" asked Lauren politely.

The woman smiled. "You must be Lauren. Come on in."

Lauren felt a little more at ease as she followed Mrs. Redding into her dilapidated house. Behind her, Paul and Christopher hoisted the cart up the unstable staircase. The floorboards creaked loudly underfoot. The house was full of old, threadbare furniture and some antique pieces that Mrs. Redding must have had for many years. On top of an upright piano in the living room sat a grouping of old family photographs.

"What would you like done first, Mrs. Redding?" Lauren asked, as she assessed the warm but rundown house.

"Anything would be an improvement. I wish I could do it myself," Mrs. Redding replied wistfully. "But I think the kitchen first, then the bathrooms and the dusting."

Lauren walked down the hall to where the boys were slouched against the cleaning cart. Christopher shot her a sullen look.

"Okay. One of you can vacuum the entire living room and dining room area," she began. "And one of you can sweep and wash the kitchen floor."

"Oh, man, do we have to?" whined Mark.

Paul and Matt laughed.

"Yes," Lauren said firmly. "And the more you complain, the more I'll find for you to do." She shoved her hands deep in the pouch pocket of her sweatshirt, hoping they wouldn't notice how nervous she was.

"Bow wow," said Mark.

Lauren tried to ignore him and fumbled with the vacuum cleaner. She could feel the heat creeping into her face as the boys eyed her. With great effort, she thrust the vacuum at Matt. Then she handed the mop and broom to Mark, and some sponges to Paul.

Mrs. Redding walked stiffly over to Lauren. "Lauren, dear, there's some trash in the backyard that needs clearing, too."

"Okay, Mrs. Redding. Christopher will be happy to do that."

Mark and Christopher laughed.

Christopher came forward, checking his watch. "Hey, listen. I'm trying to be a good sport here, but I've got to go pretty soon. I'm due down at the TV station."

Fear thickened in Lauren's throat. "You can't leave. This is your punishment."

"I don't really have time to play janitor, especially in the middle of rush," Christopher said.

"You should've thought of that before you let your guys haze that pledge last year," Lauren shot back.

Christopher pulled her out into the hall, after giving Mrs. Redding his most charming smile. "Look," he said, sticking his hands on his hips. "You know as well as I do that I shouldn't have to be part of this. I didn't haze that guy. I never even touched him."

Lauren looked him right in the eye. "It doesn't matter. You're president of ODT. You should have stopped it. The interfrat council agreed with me and that's why you got assigned this service too."

Christopher ran his hand through his hair and huffed. "All right. You want to be tough? Why don't you at least be fair at the same time? We made a mistake last year and you smeared it all over the pages of the newspaper. Now we're being nice boys. At least we should get another article in the *Journal* about how the ODT brothers are helping out old people. It's not fair that only our negative side gets publicized."

Lauren's nervousness hardened into anger. "You must be kidding!" she exploded. "If the clean-up were a voluntary thing, I'd be happy to give you guys credit for it. But this clean-up is mandatory punishment, and you've tried your best to get out of it. I don't see any reason in the world to reward you with publicity."

Christopher remained maddeningly cool and unperturbed. "Lauren, you have it all wrong."

"No, I have it all right." She thrust a toilet

brush in his hand. "Here. Mrs. Redding needs her toilet cleaned. Get busy."

From inside came the roar of the vacuum cleaner. Lauren marched angrily past Christopher and went in to check up on the other guys.

In the kitchen, Mark and Paul were laughing and barely moving the mop along the floor. Before she could yell at them, Christopher called out.

"Hey, Lauren." He stood in the living room, holding the toilet brush. "What's the best way to clean a toilet? I'm sorry, but I've honestly never done this before."

For the first time that day, Lauren actually believed him. "I'll show you."

She grabbed a tin of cleanser and led him down the hall. Christopher followed her into the bathroom, where she leaned over the toilet bowl and gave a demonstration. "Now, do you think you can handle it?"

She turned around with the brush in her hand, ready to give it to Christopher—but he was gone.

"CHRISTOPHER!" she yelled. She ran down the hall, dangling the dripping toilet brush—just in time to see Christopher jogging out the front door.

"And here we have with us tonight at the famous Rapids Hall party—the WaWaRelles, singing 'Do Wop Your Bo Wop, Baby.'"

Applause and laughter echoed across the brightly lit quad. Small, colored lanterns had been strung from tree to tree to provide light, and a long refreshment table was set up with chips, dips, and cut-up vegetables for the hungry.

"One and a-two and a-three . . ."

"I don't know the words."

"Do wop, you're my baby . . ."

Peter and his friends broke into song, parodying an old fifties tune. Then a foursome broke in, singing old advertising jingles. Finally a live salsa band called "Hot Sauce" drowned them all as it plunged into a wild number, its members rocking madly to the music.

"Hey, let's boogie!"

"What about the oldies but goodies?"

"Later, dude."

"Olé!" shouted Peter. The singer laughed and gave him the high sign.

"There's Moe, the study grind!"

"Ferd the Nerd—get your bod over here!"

People swarmed onto the lawn to dance, waving their arms wildly in the air.

"Get your elbow out of my ear!"

"Yahoo!" Brooks Baldwin wound his arm around overhead as though throwing a lasso. Next to Brooks, Melissa, in a pink warm-up suit, danced as though she were jogging in place.

It was an unusually warm evening. A soft breeze rustled the branches and caused the lanterns to send colored wands of light bobbing across the green. Peter scanned the wild mob, looking for familiar faces. There was Faith, KC's friend, dancing with a short guy from his dorm. And Phoenix, that wild man from Rapids who never wore socks. Suddenly Peter saw something out of the corner of his eye and did a double take.

"No, it couldn't be," he said out loud. "You're dreaming." He squinted his eyes, figuring they were playing tricks on him. "Too much camera work makes you crazy. It must be a mirage. Take two. . . ."

The music stopped and then he was sure. KC and Courtney were talking to Faith,

Lauren, and Dash right in front of the band. Hope blossomed inside him as he drew closer. KC's tall, confident figure was unmistakable. Nobody looked as bold and sure of herself as KC. She had a red flower pinned in her long, lush hair and was dressed rather casually. Peter smiled. He moved to the fringe of the group to get a better look.

"What are you doing here?" he heard Faith ask, as she gave KC a big hug.

"Long story," said KC, winking at Courtney.

Then Lauren and Dash turned around.

"A visit from the royal court, huh?" Dash asked with a sly smile.

Lauren was visibly shocked. "Courtney, KC. Isn't there a big party on Greek Row tonight? I saw Christopher and his buddies today. And I hope I never see them again."

"We heard *this* party would be a lot more fun," Courtney said, a little embarassed. "A big change from Greek Row."

"I guess. Don't these guys swallow goldfish whole or something?" asked Dash with a smirk.

"Gross."

"They don't do that!" cried Lauren, tickling Dash.

"Not as far as I know," said Courtney, turning pink.

KC started the introductions. "Lauren and Dash, who you know already, Melissa and Brooks, Kimberly, Freya, and Brooks's roommate, Barney Sharfenburger." Kimberly, a talented black dancer, and Freya, a German opera major, lived next door to Faith and Lauren.

"Hi."

Courtney smiled and nodded to everyone. "Nice to meet you all," she said politely.

Peter moved into a wand of light and KC suddenly turned and saw him standing just a few feet from her. Her perfect features froze.

"Peter," she whispered.

"KC."

Their eyes locked. KC averted her gaze and picked a leaf off her red cable-knit sweater.

"I thought you were a vision," he said, raking his hair back.

"You mean a nightmare?"

Peter shook his head. "KC, why do you always have to . . ."

"Hey, everybody, let's rock and roll!"

The band pumped out a hot song, and Peter suddenly became aware of the mob scene around him. Kimberly began to move to the rhythm.

"Hey, how about a dance, everyone?" Kimberly suggested.

The cluster began to break up as everyone followed Kimberly to the well-lit square of lawn in front of the band.

"Why did you come?" Peter asked KC.

She shrugged. "I wanted to."

"Yeah, but it's not really your style, is it? What happened to the frat party?"

She shrugged again. "I didn't feel like going."

"But I thought that party was one of your sorority requirements. Or did I get it wrong?"

"Are we playing twenty questions here?" KC demanded.

Peter grinned. "Just one more. Wanna dance?"

"Sure," KC said, remaining cool.

The band played a slow song. Peter's confidence grew as he slipped one arm around her back and took her hand. She put one arm around his shoulder, a little stiffly at first, as though she didn't quite want to let herself go.

"So, did you come to this party just to see me?" Peter asked, guiding her across the soft carpet of lawn.

KC flushed red. "No, I didn't. It sounded like fun, and Courtney wanted to come."

"Courtney wanted to come? I don't believe that."

"She's here. We came together," KC insisted, glancing around for the Tri Beta president.

"Seems like she'd need one of those embossed invitations before she'd go anywhere."

"You don't know Courtney very well."

Peter tightened his grip on her back and whirled her around. "Maybe not. But admit it, KC, *you* came to see *me*."

"I did not!" KC cried indignantly, wrenching herself away to arm's length.

"Yes, you did. You knew I was coming."

"Peter, you're crazy."

"And you haven't seen anything yet." He grinned; the music slowed down and he pulled her close again. "Admit it, KC. Make my day."

She sighed and placed her hands lightly on his shoulders. "Okay, I admit it. I came to see you. Happy?"

Peter wanted to freeze-frame the moment.
"You bet."

While KC was dancing with Peter, Courtney stood on the sidelines. She wasn't sure if
her burst of wildness had run dry, or if she was
just too out of place at this party to ever let go
and have a good time. She wondered if she
should have gone to the ODT party after all,
no matter what kind of rush prank they had in
mind for her girls.

But then she saw him, standing near the
band, bobbing to the music with a happy grin
on his face.

Although she hadn't wanted to admit it,
even to herself, she had come to this party to
find Phoenix. And there he was, wearing a col-
orful woven shirt over jeans and sandals. His
hair shone under the colored light and he
looked as graceful and happy as an adventurer
on his first trek.

Courtney tried to take a step toward him,
but her legs wouldn't move. What would he
think when he saw her? In her sleeveless black
dress and heels she was dressed as casually as
she knew how to dress for a party. And yet,

compared to everyone else, she might as well have been going to a prom.

He looked over. There were so many people dancing between them that she wasn't sure if he really saw her. But then he smiled, and he put his hand to his forehead as if he couldn't believe what he was seeing. He made his way over.

"I thought you were a vision," he cried, taking her arm when he reached her. He pressed her hand and her shoulder, making sure that she was real. "I thought you were a mirage."

"I'm no mirage," Courtney said, swallowing hard. The lights and music all around her were still overwhelming.

Phoenix looked at her with his warm, brown eyes and smiled. "What are you doing here?"

Courtney looked away in embarrassment. "It's an open party, isn't it?"

"Sure. But I asked some people in my dorm about you. Apparently, you're a very big deal. They said people like you get arrested for showing up at parties like this."

Courtney laughed.

"You're here, though, and that's all that matters. It's like the sun and the mountains and the rain. Don't ask too many questions about what they're up to. Just be happy for them."

Courtney smiled and they were staring at each other again.

"Do you want to dance?" Phoenix finally asked.

"Yes," she whispered. "I'd like that."

They walked over to the mass of dancers who were packed like sardines.

The first song was slow. Courtney expected to waltz or do something else very traditional, but Phoenix's dance was hard to follow, a little made-up waltz of his own with a bounce in it.

"Are you on your way someplace else?" asked Phoenix, guiding her with his strong hand in the middle of her back.

His long hair tickled Courtney's nose as they danced, and she realized she'd never danced with a boy who had long hair before. Then the band moved into a fast number, its beat throbbing in the ground.

"Come on, Courtney," Phoenix urged, clapping and stamping his feet like a country western dancer. "Swing your partner!"

The tempo of the party recharged with the

sound of the music. Courtney felt excited by the warm, night air and all the noise.

Phoenix laced his arm through hers and joined a line of dancers as they snaked their way across the green.

"Here, take a torch!" someone said, handing each of the dancers a fluorescent torch in different neon colors.

Tentatively, Courtney held her torch and marveled at the string of dancers. "This looks so beautiful!" she blurted out suddenly, kicking off her high heels as she leapt across the springy grass.

Phoenix pulled Courtney into the center of the dance area. She unclipped her hair barrette and let her blond hair fall loose across her shoulders in a golden cloud. Phoenix waved his arms in the air and whooped. Courtney spun around, colors and sounds melting together in a throbbing, dizzying whirl.

Eight

Marielle walked briskly from Langston Hall, past the crazy party on the dorm green. She was headed to the ODT frat party. As an ex-Tri Beta it was going to be a little bit awkward, but she was, after all, still Mark's girlfriend. It was the perfect opportunity to keep tabs on just what was going on in her former sorority, and if she was really lucky, she might discover a way to get back at Courtney.

Marielle suddenly stopped on the edge of the dorm green. She had just spotted somebody who didn't fit into the dorm free-for-all

—somebody wearing an elegant, black dress. No, not just somebody—Courtney Connor!

Marielle stared. Courtney was dancing, whirling around like a maniac. And who was the guy? Marielle got closer and checked him out. He had long hair and a boyish, handsome face. He looked like a hippie freshman! What in the world was Courtney doing? Wasn't she supposed to be at the ODT house?

Marielle wanted to kiss the grass. "This is my lucky day. I can't believe Courtney is so stupid—but I'm glad she's stupid. Kiss it all goodbye, Courtney."

Marielle couldn't wait to get over to the fraternity house. She raced. Her heels made crisp, staccato beats when she got on the pavement. The big houses and classy BMWs of Greek Row were a welcome sight.

As Marielle entered the ODT house, three guys were hauling a keg up the front steps.

"Got enough beer inside to soak an army," one bragged.

"Yeah, the way these rushees guzzle, we'll need it."

Marielle stepped past them and scanned the loud, crowded room for Mark. Guys in suits and girls in slinky dresses were crammed into the main reception room. The mismatched furniture was shoved up against the walls and the place smelled of perfume and spilled beer. She quickly spotted Mark standing over by the fireplace, chatting with Christopher. Marielle hurried over to them.

"What's up, Marielle?" Christopher looked casually elegant in a crisp beige suit with a pale blue shirt and tie.

Marielle smiled. "I saw something very interesting on my way over here," she gushed. "Our friend Courtney seems to have gotten sidetracked."

"We were just wondering where the ice princess was," said Mark, sitting on the arm of the couch. "She's supposed to be here."

"I'll tell you where she is." Marielle tugged at the hem of her short dress. She lowered her voice for effect. "Courtney is at the Rapids Hall party on the dorm green."

"Are you sure, Marielle?" Mark asked.

"Positive. I saw her myself. I stood there watching her dance like a wild woman."

"But Courtney doesn't know anyone over there," Christopher said.

Marielle grinned. "Apparently she does. She was dancing with some guy who looks like a freshman. And like I said, she was really dancing. Her hair was flying all over and she had her shoes off . . ."

Christopher's handsome face clouded. "That's pretty insulting. Courtney promised to help with our 'Spring Rush Puzzler.'"

"I know," Marielle cooed. The Spring Rush Puzzler was an oral trivia quiz that had been designed for rushees. Each rushee was asked a series of personal questions which they had to answer on the spot. The best part for Marielle was when the undesirable rushees had to answer their questions. In the past, she and Mark had thought up some really good ones, like, "What is your real bra size?"

"Why don't you guys ask the questions?" suggested Marielle. "I'm sure it'll turn out fine." She had a sudden idea. "Look, I just want to circulate a little." She grabbed Mark's lapels and kissed him. "I'll see you in a little while."

Mark winked.

Marielle plunged into the crowd until she found Diane, who was standing by the refreshment table, talking to a couple of rushees.

"Oh, Diane, I guess you haven't seen

Courtney," Marielle said, her voice oozing sweetness.

"No, I've been wondering where she is," Diane responded. "She was supposed to be here by now. I'm worried. Do you know anything?"

"As a matter of fact, I know exactly where Courtney is. I saw her dancing at the Rapids Hall party."

"What!" Diane said in shock.

"She was with some guy I've never seen before. He looks like a real hippie."

Diane glared and Marielle walked away feeling triumphant. She wove through the crowd, picking out the most important members of the sorority and the fraternity to talk to. Soon everyone was gossiping about Courtney's irresponsible behavior.

"I heard she ditched this party for a dorm party."

"I heard she's dating a non-Greek freshman!"

"And she didn't show up here at all tonight. That's not good."

Slipping through the crowd, Marielle felt all charged up. She heard the story repeated several more times, and knew that by the time the night was over, Courtney's escapade would have spread all over Greek Row. Nothing could have filled her with more furious energy. She passed through the reception area and climbed the stairs to Mark's room.

The person responsible for her success should be thanked. It was hard to imagine that just days ago, she had been desperate, desperate with a capital "D!" But since she'd changed her attitude and started thinking aggressively, her whole life had begun to change. She wasn't a victim anymore.

Marielle opened the door of Mark's room and switched on the light. She sat down at his desk, noting the photo of herself stuck on his bulletin board. The rest of the room was decorated with tennis trophies and photographs of tennis matches. She pulled her elegant phone book out of her bag and looked up the number for the Crisis Hotline.

Punching out the number on the phone, she smiled into the receiver.

"Springfield Crisis Hotline . . . May I help you?"

"Hello, may I please speak with W.G.?"

* * *

Winnie hung up the hotline phone and slid her feet off the desk. She wiped her hand over the back of her neck. Beads of sweat had formed there and trickled down her spine. Something about her caller was suddenly giving her the creeps. Winnie was glad that Desperate was no longer feeling like a victim, but the way she talked about how she was going to get revenge on another girl made Winnie uncomfortable.

Winnie trudged over to the water cooler and poured herself a drink. Desperate was starting to sound mean, even a little dangerous. *Maybe counseling Desperate to be assertive wasn't the best advice,* thought Winnie.

Feeling dead on her feet, Winnie gathered up her stuff and headed out of the hotline office. As she approached the campus, she could hear party sounds. Once, just the word "party" would have had Winnie dancing like a fiend, but since she and Josh had broken up, she hadn't been tempted.

She passed the dorm green, which was really rocking. The band had a spicy, Latin sound that put a little lift in Winnie's tired step. She looked at the brightly lit lanterns and saw the bobbing, dancing bodies, and guessed some of her friends would probably be there.

She walked into Forest Hall, and headed for her room. For once, the place was dead. The leftovers of some in-house party were still on the hall floor—soda cans, candy wrappers and pretzel bags.

Suddenly, Winnie glanced down the hall and saw Josh standing right outside her room. He was holding a sheet of computer paper and a pencil, looking dazed.

Her heart did a 180-degree flip at the sight of him. He turned, then smiled his quirky smile, and scratched his long, brown hair. Winnie took in every detail of his appearance, from the single earring and woven bracelet he always wore, to his faded, bleach-stained T-shirt, sweat pants, and bare feet.

"Hi. Hey, how are you?" she asked, drawing closer, her insides coiled like a wound-up spring. She motioned to the piece of paper in his hand. "Got a computer glitch?"

"I'm just working on a mindless assignment." He didn't take his eyes off her for a moment, then his gaze focused on the wall. "So, how are you?"

"Tired," Winnie said, not sure whether to

stand closer or farther away. Usually she could talk circles around him and yet suddenly she had nothing to say.

"Been to the big party?" he asked, meeting her gaze again.

"No. I have a volunteer job now on Friday nights."

"Really." He rubbed his eyes. "I didn't go to it, either. The party, I mean."

They stood there without moving for a moment. Winnie didn't want him to go. They both started talking at once.

"Say—"

"Why don't we go into my room to talk for awhile?" she suggested. "It beats standing out here in the hall. We haven't talked in so long and—"

"Okay," he blurted, starting to smile.

Winnie had so much to tell him that she felt her weariness begin to evaporate.

She opened her door, with Josh right behind her. He was so close she could feel his breath on the back of her neck. She melted, remembering what it was like to be close to him, to kiss him. . . .

But then the door swung open to reveal Mel and Brooks sitting on Mel's bed, making out again. Right away, Winnie closed the door, backing right into Josh.

"What's wrong?"

Heat flooded her cheeks. "Uh, my room's occupied. I guess my roommate and her boyfriend came home from the party early. Sorry." She groaned in frustration.

"We could go to my room," suggested Josh, backing into the hallway.

Eagerly, Winnie followed him the short distance down the hall, until they both saw the Do Not Disturb sign on his door.

Josh's eyes looked sad again. "I forgot. Mikoto's studying."

"Oh, well . . ."

Josh shrugged. "Some other time, maybe."

"Yeah, I'll see you around," Winnie said, feeling like she was coming in for a crash landing on the moon.

"Right." He opened the door of his room and disappeared.

Winnie stayed in the hall for a very long time, thinking about the moment that had come and gone.

Nine

·······················

The next morning, KC lingered in bed, feeling happy. She was thinking about Peter and the fun time they had had the night before. *Daydreaming about a guy is the kind of stuff Faith or Winnie would do,* she thought. KC was usually the sensible one of the three. The last time she had fallen for someone—Steven Garth in her business class—she had been sorry. With Steven, she had always felt on guard, as though she knew it wasn't going to work. But Peter was different. Something about him made her able to relax and talk.

She threw back the covers and got out of bed. Grabbing pants, a shirt, and a blazer, KC dressed quickly. She wanted to talk to Faith and Winnie about everything. After checking herself in the mirror, she dashed down the hall and down the stairs. Her burst of adrenaline came to a stop, though, when she opened the front door and saw someone sitting on the steps of Langston House.

"Peter! Hi."

Peter looked up, squinting at her because the sun was behind her. His oversized Fotomania T-shirt reached almost to the ragged edges of his cutoffs. In his lap was his 35mm camera and a big black camera bag sat on the step next to him. "Hi, KC."

"What are you doing here?"

"This is as good a place as any to load film."

For a minute, KC was confused. "Come on, Peter. Come clean. You came to see me."

He scrunched up his face. "Whatever gave you that idea?"

"Admit it."

He shook his head and calmly snapped the back of the camera shut, then slipped the strap over his head.

Irritated, she started across the porch and down the steps.

"Listen," he said when she had reached the bottom step.

KC stopped and waited.

"I'm going up to Hosmer Lake to shoot a few rolls of film and I thought you might like to come along."

"Really?" KC blurted out, forgetting her cool. She couldn't believe that Peter had come all the way over to Langston to ask her to go to the lake with him. This was a first.

"Anyway, don't get the idea that I'm dying of love for you, but since you took the first step coming to the party, I'm here. Do you want to go or not?"

KC was torn. "I can't. I've got to visit the Springfield Children's Clinic today," she explained. "It's the Tri Beta's charity. Then tonight I have my final rush interview."

Peter put his camera in its case and stood up. "What is it with you sorority girls? You've always got 101 socially correct things to do." He slung an arm around her shoulders, buddy-buddy style. "Don't worry about any of that. I've already taken care of it for you."

"What?"

"I talked to Phoenix after last night's party. He asked Courtney to go to the lake and she said yes. So you're off the hook with the clinic. If Courtney's going, you can go."

KC was shocked. "What! Are you sure she's going?"

"Scout's honor." He held up his fingers.

KC was still in shock. She had noticed how unbelievably cozy Courtney had been with Phoenix last evening, but she thought it wouldn't last beyond that. In a way, though, Courtney's attraction to such an earthy guy made KC like Courtney even more. "Are we going on your motorcycle?"

Peter let out a short laugh. "All four of us? No, Phoenix has a truck. We'll take The Lemon."

"Let me check with Courtney. If she's really going, then I'll go."

"She's really going," Peter said, as he hopped down the steps and pretended to take her picture. "See you soon!"

Still stunned that Courtney would miss another rush event, KC ran back inside to the ground floor pay phone, which was in the hall, right next to the floor bathroom. Her voice echoed in the empty hallway as she talked.

"Courtney, it's KC. Peter told me you were going to the lake with Phoenix today." She hesitated. "Is that true?"

"Yup. I'm going, KC, and so are you." Courtney sounded almost giddy.

"But what about the Children's Clinic?"

Courtney sighed. "I've always hated parading through that hospital with a gang of girls. The kids get embarrassed. I prefer to go by myself or with one other girl and spend a little time with just a few kids. You and I can do that together next week."

"Okay," KC breathed. "But who's going to take over for you today?"

"Don't worry, KC. Diane can take charge of the hospital visit. You and I will be back in time for dinner and the final rushee interviews. Please come to the lake."

KC stared at the phone as if it were something she'd never seen before. She still couldn't believe her ears. "Okay, Courtney. Whatever you say. Let's go!"

Thirty seconds later, Marielle peered out the bathroom door, her eyes and lips the only part of her face not covered by a black mud facial mask. She had heard everything KC had said on the phone, and she was beaming. "Miss Goody Goody Courtney is going to the lake with someone named Phoenix," she said out loud. "This is my lucky day."

She ducked back in the bathroom and started scrubbing the mud off her face. This was really fabulous: Courtney was burying herself by not showing up at another important rush event.

"I want to rub your face in it, Courtney," Marielle said.

Then she checked out her freshly scrubbed, grinning reflection in the mirror, noticing how her eyes shone with excitement. *There is nothing prettier than revenge,* she thought. Smiling to herself, she left the bathroom and hurried down the hall to her room.

"Attention fellow travelers! Fasten your seat belts and get ready for a little turbulence!"

Courtney, KC, and Peter hung on as Phoenix turned off the main highway, passed a row of cattle ranches, onto a bumpy logging road. KC and Peter were in the truckbed, while Courtney and Phoenix rode in the cab of The

Lemon, Phoenix's bright yellow pickup. Courtney hung onto the window frame to keep from being jolted into Phoenix's lap. She looked around her, noticing the ripped upholstery, the dusty dash plastered with environmental stickers, and the metal floor with a hole big enough for her to see the road going by underneath her.

"I've never ridden in a pickup before," she told Phoenix.

"Really?" His eyes left the road for a split second to look at her. He was wearing a battered straw hat, sweatshirt, cutoffs, and sandals. "It's a character-building experience." He pointed to the hole in the floor board. "We are at one with nature," he joked.

Courtney laughed. The feel of the sun against her bare arm and the wind in her hair was delicious. She breathed in the scent of pine. Just then, they hit a pothole and the truck thumped down hard on the road. A string of feathers dangling from the rear view mirror swung wildly from side to side.

"Watch out, Phoenix. You're gonna lose two passengers if you keep that up!" shouted Peter from the back.

"Sorry!" Phoenix shouted back, then broke

into wild laughter. "By the way, keep an eye out for wild bears."

"Bears?" Courtney asked alarmed. "Are there bears up here?"

Phoenix grinned. "There sure are, but as long as you don't bother them, they don't usually bother you. We're all in the same universe."

The movement of the truck flung Courtney closer to Phoenix, squashing her against his side.

"You okay?"

"Yeah, fine." Courtney pulled herself off him, feeling a little bit embarrassed.

"I'll slow down," he said.

She glanced out the window at a sheer cliff dropping down from her side of the road.

"Hey, look at the deer." He pointed at the roadside where a deer vanished in the brush. "Beautiful as a poem."

As they drove farther into the forest, Courtney became very interested in her surroundings. Squirrels raced up tree trunks, another deer crossed the road in front of them, and once she saw a rabbit. Courtney had never paid too much attention to the outdoors. Until now, her world had consisted of cities and appropriate vacation spots. She had picked U. of S. because it had an excellent international relations school, and had never really thought about its natural setting.

"Look up ahead," said Phoenix as they rounded a bend.

The scene took Courtney's breath away. Glistening from inside a bunch of tall pines was a clear blue jewel of a lake that grew larger as they approached.

"It looks like a sapphire," said Courtney.

"Yeah?" said Phoenix. "That's fairly poetic. Not very many people know about it, which is probably why it's still so beautiful."

When they got right up to the lake, Courtney was anxious to get out and see the surrounding landscape mirrored in the deep water.

Excited, everyone clambered out of the truck.

"There are some ancient Indian caves around this area," Peter said. "I'd like to go look for them. Anyone else?" He looked at KC first.

"Sure." She grinned.

"No, thanks," Phoenix said. "How about you, Courtney?"

"I think I'd like to stay here and just look at the lake," she replied.

Peter hoisted a daypack onto his shoulder and set off, with KC by his side.

"See you guys later," KC called, waving gaily.

Courtney and Phoenix stood quietly, listening to the birds and the soft lapping of the water against the shore.

"Come on. I'll show you around," Phoenix said.

Courtney followed him, stepping gingerly across the rocky ground to a trail. They crossed a stream by balancing on the dry rocks. Courtney gazed down into the water and saw a big dark fish swimming by.

"I only see fish lying on ice in the supermarket," she said.

Phoenix laughed and grabbed her hand. They hiked back to the sandy area next to the lake. Phoenix brought an Indian blanket from the back of the pickup and laid it out on the pine-needle-carpeted ground. There was no one around, and it was silent.

"See the rope swing over there?" he said, pointing it out.

The rope swing hung from a tree branch

that jutted over the lake. Beneath it was a rocky incline.

"We'll try it later, if you want. It's cosmic," he said.

Courtney sat down next to him and gazed out at the still blue lake. "Why did you want to go to U. of S. ?"

"Hmmm. I guess to find what you see here." He held his arm out in a panoramic gesture. "I love the West. I'm from Montana. I didn't want to go to a university in or near a big city." He leaned back on his elbows and chewed on the end of a pine needle. "I'm an environmental studies major. I figure I'll be able to help make the world a better place. Sounds corny, huh?"

"Not at all."

"When I'm out here, I feel like I'm at home. I'm much more comfortable in a tent or sleeping on the ground than I am in civilization. Anyway, I want to have fun and do something worthwhile."

Courtney was disarmed again.

"So tell me all about yourself. I'm listening.". Phoenix lay back on the blanket, his arms behind his head.

"Well . . ." Courtney cleared her throat.

"I grew up in Boston. My family's pretty wealthy."

"I guessed."

"My father's a doctor and my mother recently got her law degree. I'm thinking of going into international relations or law myself."

"That sounds honorable."

She smiled. "I'm an only child, so I guess I was expected to act very adult from an early age."

Phoenix smiled. "It makes me understand why you're into that sorority stuff."

Courtney examined her peach-painted nails, which seemed oddly out of place in the woods. "Tri Beta was my mother's sorority and she loved it. I joined because she wanted me to. I've always done basically what my parents expected of me."

"Ever think of breaking out and doing what *you* want to do?" he asked.

Courtney smiled at him. "Once in a while."

Phoenix reached up and tugged on a strand of her golden hair. She didn't know why she suddenly felt so attracted to him, but she also wanted to hold herself back. She wanted to change a little, not transform her entire life.

All she really knew was that right then, she didn't want to be anywhere else on earth.

Phoenix smiled. Then he quickly stood up and stretched. "It's getting warm." Without another word, or a hint of hesitation, he started to undress.

"Wh-what are you doing?" Courtney gasped.

"It's hot and the water looks great. I don't know about you, but I'm going for a swim." He suddenly stood in front of her, wearing nothing but his undershorts. Courtney felt like she was dreaming again. "I'm off." Phoenix turned, loped over to the rocks, and started to climb up to the rope swing. When he reached a good height, he swung far out across the water.

"YAHOOOOO!"

Suddenly, he let go and plunged feet first into the lake. The sound cracked the silence.

Courtney tensed, wondering if he was okay. Then Phoenix's head surfaced. He was grinning. "Come on in, the water's great!" he shouted.

Courtney glanced over at the rope swing in fear. Something inside her wanted to swing, too. But what if she smashed against the rocks? She sat very still and deliberated. Phoenix's enthusiasm was infectious, and the water looked inviting. Plus, there was no one around.

Phoenix went on the rope swing again, and this time his laughter echoed off the rocks.

Courtney had never done anything like this before, and she suspected this might be her first and last chance. "Oh, what the heck," she said to herself, stripping down to her lace panties and bra. She folded her clothes and laid them neatly on a big rock, then tentatively walked over to the rope. As she looked down the rocky slope, her heart filled up with paralyzing fear.

"Courtney, swing way out over the lake before you let go!" hollered Phoenix.

She nodded, a stiff smile stuck on her face. Clutching the rope, she backed up as far as she could, and swung forward. Her legs curved up around the rope, her hands clenching the stiff, prickly surface. The air whooshed against her body.

As she swung out over the center of the lake, she heard Phoenix shout, "Let go now!"

Courtney immediately let go and felt herself fall. "Ahhhhhhh!" she screamed, plunging into the water. *Whoooosh*. She was under the surface, and surprisingly she wasn't afraid. She popped up, laughing, and felt as if every rule, every polite restriction in her life had suddenly broken away.

Phoenix laughed with her. "Now that's being one with nature," he said, holding his hand out to slap. The slap started a splashing game. Phoenix swam after her. Courtney made a scoop with her hand and used it to splash him back. He slipped his arms around her waist and lifted her out of the water, then dunked her. She giggled, then dived and swam under the surface, so she could surprise Phoenix and dunk him right back.

Ten

....

Marielle parked her Saab on the logging road, then hiked the rest of the way up to Hosmer Lake in her high-heeled shoes. When she had first thought of following Phoenix's truck, she had never guessed it would be as hard as this. How was she to know he had a four-wheel drive that would take him right up to the lake?

To make things worse, she had dressed to meet Mark for a date, and now her panty hose were being ripped to shreds and her bright red designer suit was getting torn.

Angrily, Marielle yanked a twig out of her

hair and charged ahead. The lake was coming into view, but there didn't seem to be anyone around.

A spider crawled up Marielle's hand. Frantically, she shook her hand to get it off, her charm bracelet jingling noisily. Then she ran, her heels sinking into the mossy, wet ground.

At that moment, she saw something in the water. And then she heard laughter. She started walking slowly until she got right up to the edge of the forest. In the distance she could make out two people swimming. She drew closer still. There, in the water, was Courtney.

Courtney's long, blond hair snaked down her back and hung wetly in her eyes. She got out of the water. Marielle couldn't believe her eyes. Courtney was in her bra and panties! She watched open-mouthed as Courtney climbed up some rocks, grabbed a rope, and swung out over the water. Next, Courtney was having a water fight with the dorm freshman, Phoenix—and he was in his undershorts! This was too good to be true!

Marielle snuck around the edge of the forest to where Courtney and Phoenix had left their clothes. She saw some black cases next to a couple of windbreakers. Slipping off her charm bracelet, she lowered herself to her hands and knees and crawled over. She opened one of the cases and smiled. Inside was a 35mm camera. She remembered that Peter, the guy KC was with, was a photographer.

Marielle had no idea where Peter and KC had gone, but she decided to hurry before they got back. She dug into the black camera case and found a telephoto lens, which she screwed onto the front of the camera. There were five shots left on the roll. It looked kind of complicated to operate, but then she saw the button marked "automatic," and switched to that setting. She moved closer to the water and positioned herself behind a big rock.

Marielle clicked away, getting shots of Courtney going off the rope swing, and splashing and dunking Phoenix, until the camera was out of film. Marielle snapped open the back, took out the roll of film, and dropped it in her pocket.

Crouched low, Marielle hurried back through the woods, grinning to herself. "Now I have enough evidence to completely ruin you, Courtney Connor."

* * *

"Hot chocolate . . . just what I need," Faith said, that evening as she took a cupful from the vending machine.

"A little sugar rush sounds good to me," agreed Winnie, who was juggling brownies and rushing for a table.

"*Anything* sounds good to me right now," said KC as she followed her friends to a dorm snack bar table, sipping a soda. "Anything that's bad for me."

"So, how did your big nature hike go, KC?" asked Faith, opening a copy of a play script, but not looking at it.

"It was wonderful," KC said with a relaxed smile.

"Wonderful? That's all you're going to tell us? Who do you think we are, your adviser?" teased Winnie.

KC grinned and took a piece of Winnie's brownie. "Peter and I took a hike up to some of the Indian caves around Hosmer Lake. It was great. What more do you want me to say?"

"Oh, how about romantic?" cried Winnie.

"Well, it wasn't romantic," said KC, looking off with a happy, relaxed expression. "Noth-

ing happened, we just had a great time to-
gether. We talked about school and we hiked."
She grinned, "It was just great. Courtney and
Phoenix went, too."

"Courtney and Phoenix Cates?" whispered
Winnie. "I know him from a few dorm parties. They make the weirdest couple I've ever
heard of."

"What about the Children's Clinic visit?
Faith asked. "I thought all the Tri Beta sisters
and rushees were going there this afternoon."

"Well, actually they did," KC admitted.
"Courtney and I will just go by ourselves next
week. She didn't seem to think it was a big
deal. Anyway, my final rush interview went
well." KC sighed. "I'm so glad that's over
with. The pledge roster will be posted tomorrow morning."

"Another big night on Geek Row," Winnie
joked, grabbing her neck and pretending to
gag.

Faith leaned forward with a frown. "I'd be
careful if I were you, KC."

KC looked puzzled. "Why? I'm finally almost in the Tri Betas and I'll never have to go
through rush again."

"KC," Faith insisted. "I heard some gossip."

"What?"

Faith propped her elbows on the tabletop. "I was standing in the dinner line, and I overheard some rushees talking about Marielle and Courtney. It seems Marielle is telling all the Tri Beta rushees that Courtney acted irresponsibly by skipping the ODT party. She's encouraging them to stand up for themselves and not to be victims of a destructive president."

Winnie knocked over her empty soda can and it clattered to the floor. "Victims?"

"Courtney?" KC asked. "But she's the best president they could have."

"Marielle told the girls they should be assertive about protecting their future sorority by making sure only the best people stayed in it. Only if they do that, she said, will Tri Beta remain the top sorority on Greek Row."

"Assertive?" cried Winnie.

Faith turned to her. "Winnie, what's wrong?"

"C-could you like, run that by me one more time?" Winnie asked, dragging a hand through her spiked hair.

"Marielle's trying to turn everyone against

Courtney," explained KC. "But I wonder why. I mean, what difference does it make to her now? Marielle's already been kicked out, and they'll never let her back in."

"Maybe it's just plain viciousness," Faith suggested.

"Or revenge," said KC.

Winnie wanted to scream. The words Marielle had used, "victim" and "assertive," triggered an alarm inside her. "Hey, guys. I'm due down at the hotline in about fifteen minutes," she said, grabbing her stuff. "See you later."

"Okay."

"Later, Win."

Winnie raced out into the cool night air. Clouds hung heavily overhead, dark and threatening. The tree branches around the quad were partially illuminated by the dorm lights, making them look like big claws. Clutching her kimono close to her to keep out the chill, Winnie jogged along the streets toward the Crisis Hotline office. When it was finally in sight, she made a run for the door, and plunged inside.

No one looked up when she rushed in. They were all glued to their phones. Winnie found an empty desk and dropped her carpet-bag next to it. She started to take off her kimono when the phone rang. She answered it.

"Hi, I'm Carolyn and I'm having problems with my boyfriend," said the high-pitched voice on the other end.

"Hi, Carolyn. What's the problem?" asked Winnie.

"He doesn't listen to me."

So Winnie listened . . . and listened . . . and listened until Carolyn felt better and said goodbye.

Cradling the phone against her ear, Winnie took the next call.

"Hello. This is W. G. May I help you?"

"Hi. This is Desperate. I'm so glad you're there, because I'm real excited. Hey, maybe I should call myself 'Excited' instead of Desperate, now."

"It's up to you."

"Well, you'll just never guess what I've done."

Winnie shuddered. "Tell me."

"I've gotten back at that girl who ruined my life. This time I'm ruining her. She'll never be able to set foot on this campus again without embarrassment." Desperate lowered her voice so that it sounded like a hiss. "I have evidence that will expose her." She laughed nastily. "And when I say expose, I really mean expose."

Recognition washed over Winnie like a giant wave. Marielle Danner! Winnie bit her lip, as her suspicions were confirmed. More than anything, she wanted to tell Marielle off, to give Desperate advice that would zilch her plans.

"How goes it, Winnie?" asked Teresa Gray as she strolled by.

Winnie waved her fingers and managed a smile, but the sight of Teresa zoomed the message home to her: DO YOUR JOB.

The horrible reality hit her: she had sworn an oath of confidentiality and she had a professional obligation to help anyone who called. She had to remain supportive—but never judgmental—no matter what. Suddenly her hand felt like a lump of ice holding the receiver. She felt pulled in opposite directions by her professionalism and her intuition. Why couldn't they both be telling her the same thing?

"W.G. . . . are you there?"

"Yes, yes, I'm here, Desperate."

"I thought you'd be so proud of me for getting my life back on track. Excited with me."

Gritting her teeth and closing her eyes, Winnie forced herself to speak. "Yes, Desperate. I'm happy for you. Very, very happy."

That same evening, Lauren hurried off campus toward Dash's boarding house. The sky was black with storm clouds and a thick fog made it hard to see. She made a detour to Bickford Lane because she wanted to deliver some food to Mrs. Redding. At the door of the old house, Lauren knocked loudly. Mrs. Redding appeared, and looked surprised to see her.

"Lauren! What a treat! Come in." The elderly woman ushered her inside.

"I can't stay long, Mrs. Redding. I just wanted to give you this." Lauren pulled out some boxes of cereal and a bag of apples, all she could afford on her maid's salary.

"Oh, thank you," said Mrs. Redding gratefully.

Lauren left quickly, because she was a little embarrassed, but when she stepped onto the street again, her embarrassment turned to confusion.

Bright lights washed over the houses on Bickford Lane. There was a crowd of people and an official-looking van parked out front.

Afraid that someone had had an accident, Lauren ran toward the lights, trying to figure out what was happening. She stopped when she saw TV cameras. As she drew closer, Christopher, Mark, Paul, and Matt came into view. They were standing on the porch of one of the houses, wearing suits and ties and looking earnestly into a camera.

Christopher held a broom. "Make sure you get Mark, me, and the mop," he told the crew.

With sinking realization, Lauren saw that Christopher had gone ahead and gotten what he wanted. Through his internship at the TV station, Christopher had arranged a news spot featuring the ODTs helping the people on Bickford Lane.

Lauren clenched her fists in anger and charged through the thick fog to Dash's place.

"If only the public knew that those so-called 'good-hearted' boys have hearts made out of

slime!" she muttered, through clenched teeth.
"You may have won this round Christopher,
you creep!" Lauren railed under her breath.
"But I'll win the next one."

Eleven

"The next rushee on our list is KC Angeletti." It was Sunday morning and Courtney was sitting happily at the head of the long dining room table of the Tri Beta house. She was surrounded by all her sorority sisters, as they voted on which of the rushees would be asked to pledge.

It was a very solemn, very serious, very important occasion—one critical to each girl who had gone through rush. In spite of that, Courtney was feeling anything but subdued. Her good spirits threatened to bubble over. Her heart was so full, so free and light, that every single girl on her list seemed to have terrific possibilities.

"All for KC?" she said.

Every hand went up.

Courtney thrust a fist into the air. "Yes! With my vote, it's unanimous."

She put a checkmark next to KC's name and hummed an old rock song that Phoenix had sung to her on the way home from the lake. Then she grinned again at the room full of her Tri Beta sisters. They seemed to be slightly confused by her behavior.

"Courtney," hinted Diane, who was sitting right next to her. "Don't we need to take an opposed vote just as a formality?"

Courtney giggled. "Okay. All opposed?" Her eyes darted around the room. "See, no one is opposed," she said to Diane, who nodded.

Courtney continued down the list. There were a few more unanimous yeses, as well as some heated discussions about other girls' grades, their parents, personalities, and looks. Courtney sat with her crazy smile, voting yes on all the girls she liked, no matter what their backgrounds or their looks, and voting no on the girls she didn't like, in spite of their backgrounds and their looks.

"Okay, last one," Courtney announced, tapping her papers on the tabletop. "Lisa Jean McDermett."

"I don't know," whined Marcia Tabbert, a red-haired beauty who tended to be a snob. "Lisa Jean is such a bookworm. Boring clothes. Dull, dull, dull."

"She's also a mathematics major with a 3.7 average," Courtney reminded her. "We can change a girl's clothes, but we can't make her smarter. I say Lisa Jean's exactly the kind of girl we need."

"Tell me about it," piped up another sister. "I could sure use a math tutor living in the house. Especially during finals."

"I liked her!" another sister said. "She's got a good sense of humor."

A fourth sister raised her hand. "Lisa Jean also plays volleyball, so she could help us on our team."

By the time they voted, Lisa was almost as popular as KC. Her name was dropped into the yes pile, which Courtney handed to Diane. After the meeting, Diane was going to type up the list of girls who had made the final

cut and post it for all the anxious rushees to
see.

"Now we should all get the house cleaned
up and ready for tonight," Courtney said.
"Our rushees have put in a lot of effort this
week, and I don't want them to be disap-
pointed in anything about the Tri Betas."

The girls applauded as they all pushed back
their chairs and began to move away from the
table.

"Everybody should have a great time tonight," Courtney said, beaming. Diane
agreed. The event involved new girls coming
for a celebration, and then all the houses on
the row opening their doors to greet one an-
others' new brothers and sisters.

It meant a lot of work, though. Courtney
led the way to the living room to start the
house cleanup. She still felt so fizzy, so free
and loose, that she could have slid down the
stairway banister or jumped on the sofas. Instead, she kept humming Phoenix's rock song
as she helped push back furniture and pick up
magazines and books.

All the girls got busy, bringing out feather
dusters and vacuum cleaners, spray wax, and
brooms. Meanwhile, Courtney put a tape into

the stereo, one she'd never noticed before on the well stocked music shelf: Chuck Berry's Greatest Hits.

She was actually dancing and singing along, when the front door burst open. At that moment, someone shut off the music and all heads seemed to turn in the same direction.

That's when Courtney finally saw the girl who had entered the foyer. Marielle was smiling triumphantly, obviously waiting for one of her ex-housemates to make her feel at home.

"Marielle, what are you doing here?" Courtney finally asked. "I didn't expect to see you in this house again."

"I have to speak to you about something, Courtney," Marielle answered. "It's quite important."

Some of the Tri Beta girls put down their brooms and dust rags. All of them continued to stare.

"We have a big night tonight, Marielle. I'll speak with you after we've finished cleaning up," Courtney said firmly.

"I don't think you want to wait that long, Courtney."

"What do you mean?"

Marielle walked into the center of the living

room so that no one would miss a word. "I have information about a certain swim at a certain mountain lake," she said, putting her hands on her hips, so that her charm bracelet jangled. "It's important information. If you don't want to hear it, I can tell everyone else on Greek Row instead."

Instantly, Courtney felt as if she'd been punched in the stomach. She tried to maintain her dignity, but it took her utmost control. "Everyone, please keep working," she told her sisters. "We won't have much time to do anything once the lists are posted and open house begins." She glanced at Diane. "I'll be back down in a few minutes," she assured her.

Courtney marched up the stairs, followed by Marielle. Once they were safely behind the door of Courtney's bedroom, Marielle sat down on Courtney's bed as though she owned it.

"I have something to show you," Marielle said, digging in her eelskin bag. "These just *happened* to come into my hands yesterday."

She handed a packet of photographs to Courtney, who began leafing through the stack. The awful feeling in Courtney's stomach grew worse. She began to feel faint. Each picture was worse than the next. All of them showed Courtney swimming at the lake with Phoenix, and it was obvious they were wearing nothing but their undergarments. Courtney had the strange feeling that she was looking through scenes of a nightmare, one that wouldn't let her wake up.

She tried to keep her composure. "Where did you get these, Marielle?"

"I don't have to tell you."

Suddenly Courtney lost her patience. She began to tear the photos into tiny pieces, but Marielle acted as if it were a joke. "I'm not a moron, Courtney," she insisted. "I have the negatives."

Slowly, Courtney absorbed the impact of what Marielle had said. It was called blackmail. She sunk into her desk chair and stared blankly at her computer.

"What do you want from me?"

Marielle crossed her legs and placed her hands in her lap, her smile broadening. "I used to want to get back into this sorority," she admitted, "but now that you've ruined the reputation of this house forever, I'm not sure I want to be part of it." Marielle sighed deeply. "On the other hand, I also don't want to see my poor ex-sisters become victims of your irresponsible behavior."

Courtney took a deep breath. "Marielle, what do you want?" she exploded.

Marielle remained unimpressed. She got up and flounced about the tiny room, picking up Courtney's stuffed animals and tinkling the charms on her bracelet. "It's bad enough that you can't be bothered to visit your own house's charity," was her next comment. "And you certainly don't have time for fraternity parties at the ODT house anymore. Everyone already knows how much you've slipped, but what's going to happen when these photos are all over Greek Row?"

"MARIELLE, WHAT DO YOU WANT ME TO DO!" Courtney demanded, her anger and fear mixing, until she began to tremble.

Marielle sighed again, relishing Courtney's agitation.

"I'll tell you what I want from you, Courtney," she answered, her twangy voice becoming serious. "You took something from me that I really valued—my membership in this house. Well, now that I've learned to be a little more assertive, I want you to understand what I'm going through. I want you to step down as Tri Beta president."

Courtney looked stunned.

"If you resign as president, I'll burn the negatives," Marielle continued. "Otherwise, this house will be the laughingstock of Greek Row."

Courtney swallowed, but didn't say anything. Marielle pressed her. "You're not the only one who'll suffer, Courtney." She moved toward the door. "Think about your friend KC. She worked hard to climb her way into the Tri Betas, didn't she? What good will it do her if this house becomes a dirty joke? If you can't do it for yourself, Courtney, do it for Kahia Cayanne." Marielle made the real name KC's hippie parents had given her sound like two dirty words.

Courtney slumped over her desk.

"I'm going back to my lovely dorm room now," Marielle said in parting. "I'll wait one hour for your decision. If I haven't heard from you by then, and you haven't assured me that you will step down as president, I will pass those revealing photos to all of Greek Row before your welcome speech tonight.

You'll be an embarrassment to this whole house."

Courtney felt so dizzy that she thought she might collapse. It took real effort to steady herself.

Marielle sensed her near victory. "I can promise you one thing," she gloated, as she opened the door. "Once those photos are circulated up and down this street, no one will look at Courtney Conner the same way again."

Marielle blew Courtney a mock kiss and disappeared down the staircase. Her footsteps sounded like funeral music to Courtney, but it wasn't that simple. Courtney knew it wasn't just her life Marielle was talking about, it was every single Tri Beta, too. It was all the girls who had trusted her to be the leader of the sorority.

Courtney felt helpless. She didn't know who to turn to, or where to go, or what she would say if anyone ever saw those photographs. In fact, the only thing she knew how to do at that moment, was sit in her room and begin to cry.

Twelve

Winnie zoomed up the Coleridge Hall stairs, mouth open wide in imitation of some first floor opera singer, whose aria echoed through the halls of the dorm. When Winnie reached the second floor, she rapped loudly on Faith's door.

Faith let her in and laughed when she saw Winnie hitting her high C and waving her arms. "Gee, I wondered who it was," she teased.

"Just me, old big mouth," said Winnie, crumpling dramatically onto the floor. "Just heard the big news from Geek Row—wanna know what it is?"

Faith calmly sat down at her desk chair, curling her feet underneath her. "Tell me."

"In a minute. News like this deserves a big build-up."

"Just come out with it," Faith demanded, flinging a wadded-up piece of notepaper at her. "Did KC get in?"

Winnie batted the paper back. "KC's name was on the Tri Beta pledge list!"

"Great!" said Faith. She got up and gave Winnie a celebratory hug. "I've been worried since I heard that gossip at dinner the other night. Any other news?"

"I don't know. People seem to be talking a lot, but I'm not the type they want to talk to. The news about KC was all I could get," Winnie joked. Anyway, I think a victory party for KC is in order. What do you say?"

Faith smiled. "Anything for KC."

"We'll have it in my room," Winnie suggested. "Just us three and Lauren. Pineapple pizza or something else totally gross. Okay?"

"Sounds good to me."

Winnie smiled. "Great. I'll let you get back

to work, but promise me you won't study until the petunias bloom."

"Wouldn't think of it," Faith laughed.

"See you around three, then," she said on her way out. In the hall, she started imitating the opera singer again, but stopped when she got outside Coleridge and realized people were looking at her. She began jogging at a fast clip, jumping over a bench and swerving to avoid a couple wrestling each other on the grass.

While she ran, she thought about KC's acceptance into the Tri Betas. It made her feel a little better about having given advice to Marielle.

"Maybe I should've told Marielle exactly what I thought, even if it meant being unprofessional," Winnie muttered to herself, as she approached her dorm.

She bounded up the front steps into the Forest Hall lobby, where some jocks were having a squirt gun fight. When she got past them, she kept thinking. *"All I did was tell Marielle to be assertive, not to be a victim,"* Winnie reasoned. *"That's all good advice. How was I supposed to know I was giving good advice to a rotten human being?"*

Winnie slowed down when she neared her room, then dug in her pocket for a key. That was when she heard giggling coming from inside. Winnie froze. She didn't have to be told that Brooks and Melissa were at it again.

"No!" Winnie groaned.

She was tempted to knock the door down, and scream her lungs out, but instead she concentrated on taking deep breaths.

Then there was another loud giggle. Winnie couldn't stand it anymore. She wondered if she should call the hotline herself and ask what to do about this problem. *Wait!* Winnie suddenly interrupted her own thoughts. *Maybe I should take my own advice. All this time she had been giving Marielle sound advice, while she had been letting herself turn into a royal victim and wimp.*

She quickly stuck her key in the door and opened it, letting it bang against the wall. Mel and Brooks were lying on *her* bed, tickling each other.

"Hi, guys. It's me, long lost roommate Winnie," she stated. "Also known as homeless Winnie."

"Hi, Winnie," Mel said between hysterical giggles. Brooks waved.

Winnie cleared her throat noisily. "Look, I know you guys don't remember that I'm an occupant of half of this room, but I am. And I'm standing at the foot of my very own bed."

Melissa giggled loudly but came up for air. "What?"

Winnie cupped her hands around her mouth and shouted: "May I have your attention please?"

Brooks finally sat up and blinked at her innocently through tousled blond curls.

Melissa finally pushed her shoulder-length red hair out of her eyes and rolled away from Brooks.

"You guys have taken over this room," Winnie said matter-of-factly. "And it's not fair."

Melissa looked confused.

"Mel, I can't study. I can't find a place to talk to Josh. Right now I want to get this room ready for a party. Now, either you and Brooks can help, or you can find someplace else to go this afternoon."

Mel looked at her in total shock. "It's my room, too, Winnie," she said defensively.

"Mel, you guys monopolize this room," Win declared. "You know that word 'roommate'? Mates are supposed to share. We're not sharing this room, because you're sharing it with Brooks!"

Melissa blushed as she looked at Brooks, and then back to Winnie. "I'm sorry, Winnie," she finally said. "I didn't realize we were making you uncomfortable. Why didn't you say something before?"

Winnie raised her hands. "I guess I didn't have the nerve."

Melissa smiled and pulled Brooks to his feet. "Why don't we go over to your room," she said.

Brooks nodded. "Sorry, Win."

"It's okay."

Melissa pulled her track sweatshirt off a hanger, while Brooks somewhat sheepishly walked out into the hallway. "I really am sorry, Winnie. I just didn't know."

"Well, now you do," Winnie said as she watched them go. When they were gone she fell onto her bed in triumph.

"I DID IT! How about that? It wasn't so bad, now, Winnie, was it? If you can do that, what else can you do?"

She sat up and thought of Josh. Ninety thousand times a day she thought of Josh. She had to do something about it. But what? All she knew was that she was on a lucky streak. The time to act was now.

She glanced at her reflection in the mirror, re-spiked her short hair, and left the room. The hall was empty. Winnie took a deep breath, walked a few yards, and knocked on Josh's door.

After several nervous seconds, the door opened. Josh stood there, his eyes wide. "Win," he said.

Seeing him filled Winnie with love. She smiled as her eyes lingered on his blue earring, his long, dark hair, his sad but surprised eyes and tall, slender body. That's when it happened. Without any preparation or thought, Winnie flung her arms around Josh's neck and pressed her mouth to his. At first he didn't respond, but then she felt his body ease, his lips part, and his arms wind themselves around her with almost frantic urgency.

When the kiss ended and she pulled back to see his reaction, Josh was staring at her in shock.

Painful memories pressed against Winnie's throat. She bit her lip, as tears began to well up in her eyes. "I had to do that," she said, her voice trembling.

Josh was still silent, staring at her as if he were memorizing her features.

"I don't know what's going to happen next," Winnie said, wiping the tears with her forearm. She took a step away from him, then reached back to touch him with her hand. "But I had to take the first step," she admitted.

He touched her hand lightly.

Winnie ran back to her room, but turned back to look at him when she reached her door. Josh was still standing there, gazing at her, a tear rolling down his cheek, but a big smile on his face.

"Pineapple pizza. Gee Win, what can I say?"

"Don't say anything, KC. Just eat it. Yum, yum."

"I think it's good," said Faith, pulling on a strand of mozzarella.

"I guess I'm just not hungry."

"Come on, KC," Lauren urged. "You've worked hard to get into Tri Beta, and now that you're accepted you should celebrate."

It was late that afternoon. The girls were gathered in Winnie's room. KC could tell that Winnie was flying high. Lauren and Faith were cheerful too. Still, KC couldn't get her spirits up.

"Thanks for the party," she said. "I really appreciate it. In fact, I'm honored. I just wish I was in a better mood."

"Well, you've certainly had a better week than I have," Lauren admitted.

Faith shook her head. "I can't believe that Christopher got away with getting his fraternity on the news and making them look like guys with hearts of gold."

"Oh well," Winnie sighed. "Real life is like that. The good guys don't always win. Sometimes the bad guys just end up getting all the breaks."

KC put her untouched piece of pizza back in the box. She was already dressed for that night's Tri Beta welcome party and brushed crumbs off her pleated skirt.

"KC, are you okay?" asked Faith.

KC tensed. "I'm worried," she finally admitted. "When I went to check the pledge list, I heard a couple of girls say that Courtney's presidency is in trouble."

"Really?" Winnie asked with concern.

KC sighed. "I guess something is going to happen tonight. Marielle's been spreading rumors about some kind of scandal. It looks like everyone on the row is going to stop by the Tri Beta house to see what's going on."

"What are you going to do?" Faith asked.

"I thought I could help Courtney somehow, but I don't think I really can." KC nervously picked at the pizza box. "You know, this is weird, and you probably won't believe it. All year, I've wanted to be a Tri Beta. It's been so important to me to get into the classiest, most exclusive sorority on campus."

"Well, that's because you're about the classiest, most exclusive person we know," Faith teased.

"Also the preppiest," Winnie said with a giggle. "Lauren used to have you beat, but not anymore."

All of them laughed, but it couldn't cover up KC's worry. She got up and started to pace. "But you know what?" KC questioned, even though she had the answer herself. "That's not really so important anymore."

"What isn't?"

"Getting into the sorority."

The three girls were stunned into silence. KC could hardly ignore their looks. In fact it spurred her on. "It's true. Being a Tri Beta isn't everything to me anymore. Since I've gotten to know Courtney better she's become a real friend. If she can't be president of the Tri Betas, I don't know if I want to be a pledge."

Winnie stared in disbelief.

"But it's what you've wanted," said Lauren.

KC gazed at her friends with tears in her eyes. "I mean it. If Courtney isn't president of the Tri Betas, then I don't even want to join. Is that clear?"

"I'll say it's clear," Faith nodded. "Sounds to me like you've made up your mind."

"And when KC makes up her mind," Winnie laughed, "watch out!"

KC folded her arms. She meant what she had said, but it would be painful to give up something she wanted so badly.

Thirteen

"**I**'ll never show my face on this street again," Courtney said as she stared out her bedroom window.

Dusk had fallen and the sororities and fraternities were already opening their doors for the open house welcoming new pledges. Since Marielle's visit that morning, Courtney hadn't budged from her room. She hadn't answered her phone. Except for dressing for the party, she had spent the day staring out her window and waiting for her world to come to an end.

Voices wafted up from the street and Courtney couldn't help but listen.

"Did you hear about Courtney Conner? I heard she ditched a bunch of rush events, but that's not all."

"Really?"

"What else?"

"This is the new hot scoop. I didn't even see these until twenty minutes ago. Look at these pictures!"

"Oh my God!"

"No."

"What was she thinking of? She's supposed to be president of the best sorority on the row. What a joke."

"Where did you get them?"

"From some guys at ODT. But you can get them anywhere. Everyone on the Row has copies."

"How will Courtney ever show her face tonight?"

"Maybe she won't."

"Besides, who cares about her face anymore? She's been showing a lot more than that!"

The laughter got so loud that Courtney wanted to break her window and shower the girls with pieces of glass. She began to sob, then went over and lay down on her bed.

"What am I going to do!" she wailed. "I should have just told Marielle that I would step down. Now I'll have to step down anyway, and the whole house will be humiliated!"

Courtney thought about KC and all the other rushees. She thought about Diane and all her sisters. She wanted to strangle Marielle.

"Maybe I should never have been friendly with Phoenix, especially not during rush. I should have followed every rule and never let Faith and Winnie help that first day at Mill Pond. Then maybe I would never have hit my head, and never have met Phoenix. . . ."

She looked out her window again. The crowd had grown bigger and they were all huddled together, probably over copies of her photographs. She felt like she was going to throw up.

"Isn't this where she lives?" a guy outside said.

Someone else whistled. "Hey Courtney, let us see some of those lacy underthings again. Wooooooo."

"Cut that out, Paul," a girl complained. "Don't be such a jerk. So she went swimming in her underwear. Big deal."

"I'm not being a jerk," Paul argued. "I

didn't pose in my underwear for everybody to see."

"And we're all glad of that," the girl tossed back. "You wouldn't be a pretty sight in your underwear."

Courtney wanted to run, but she didn't know how she would get off the row without running into people.

"If only I could talk to someone," she said. "If only I could magically beam KC in here and ask her advice. Or Phoenix. If only I could talk to Phoenix."

"Phoenix," she argued with herself. "Maybe this whole thing is his fault. No, it's my fault. No, it's the world's fault." She sat up and ran her fingers through her hair. "I don't know."

The voices from the street drifted up again.

"Well, it's almost time for the welcome party. I can't wait to see if Courtney has the nerve to show her face."

"I wouldn't join now if I were a new girl. Would you?"

"Are you kidding?"

"I'd still join," said a dissenting voice.

"Well, you're a fool," another girl spat back.

"I'm the fool," Courtney said, standing up and throwing her study sweater over her party dress. "And I'm an even bigger fool to stick around here and listen to this."

She opened her door a crack and checked the hall. The coast was clear. She headed down the hall to a back staircase. Sneaking behind the kitchen, the odor of cooking reached her nose, making her feel dizzy. Light rock music was playing in the living room, and she could hear people start to come in from the street.

"Well hello," she heard Diane greeting guests in the living room. "Come in. No, Courtney isn't down yet, but she'll join us soon, I hope."

Courtney snuck through the kitchen and out the back door. But even as she hurried through the little back garden and along the hedge, she didn't know where she was going.

I have to get away from here, she thought, starting to cry again.

And that was when it jelled inside her head —the only solution. *"I'll lie,"* she told herself. *"I'll tell everyone that I suffered memory loss and personality change when I hit my head. That's why I swam in the lake and jumped off that rope and let someone take those pictures. Then I'll say*

I'm all better, and I'll just go back to being the Courtney I used to be."

Clusters of girls had gathered on the sidewalk, talking and laughing.

"Yeah, I wonder if she'll get brought up in front of the sorority council?"

"Of course she will."

"The guy who was swimming with her is a freshman."

"I heard that he's a hippie!"

Courtney considered walking up to the girls and explaining. The gossip was like arrows being shot at her. Each one stung her and she felt like she was going to die from the humiliation and pain. Finally, she ran down sorority row, not sure where she was going until she passed Luigi's Pizza and the record store. Turning onto campus, she raced by the football stadium. It looked dark and eerie, as did the library, the student union, and the lawns.

Out of breath, Courtney finally found herself at the edge of the dorm green. She walked along until she reached Rapids Hall. Without hesitating, she flung the front door open. Two boys stopped in mid-sentence when they saw her run in.

"Whoa!"

"You okay?" asked one of them.

"Could you tell me where Phoenix Cates's room is?" she asked breathlessly.

"Room 205—right down this hall."

Courtney ran down the plain, beige hall to room 205. When she got there, she pounded on the door.

Phoenix answered. He was wearing unlaced hiking boots, a T-shirt which said Go Climb a Rock, and shorts. His eyes took in her tear-stained face and moved aside to gesture her inside.

"Courtney. What's wrong?"

She followed him inside and burst into fresh tears. Through a film of water, she checked out his room—Sierra Club posters were all over his side of the room, a backpack was propped against the closet door, and camping equipment was all over the floor. On his desk was a stack of botany and environmental science textbooks, seashells, and geodes.

Phoenix pulled out a chair for her to sit down.

"I never should have talked to you," she raved. "Why did you ever bother me at the hospital? Why did you ever take me to that stupid lake? I'll never be able to show my face on Greek Row again!" She burst into sobs, curling her thin body over her stomach.

Phoenix leaned over and pushed the hair away from her face. "Tell me what happened!"

"You won't understand," she said, tears streaming down her face. "It's all your fault."

Phoenix sat down in another chair facing her, then he reached over and pulled a wad of tissues out of a box.

Courtney blew her nose and wiped her eyes.

"Can you tell me now?" He watched her with concern, his knees touching hers.

She took a deep breath, but her sobs started all over again. She talked through them. "Someone took pictures of me at the lake and is spreading them all over Greek Row. I've become a dirty joke."

He held her arms. "Who would do something like that?"

"A girl who used to be in my sorority. She said that if people saw my pictures, the reputation of the Tri Betas would be ruined—I would be ruined. She was trying to blackmail me into stepping down from the presidency."

Phoenix shook his head, his handsome face clouding with pain.

"But I didn't say I'd do what she wanted so she passed out the pictures. I wish I could die, but I have to face everyone and somehow make them understand." Courtney clutched her wad of tissues. "I think I've figured out a plan to handle this mess."

"What?" Phoenix asked.

Courtney shuddered. "I can say that I sustained a personality change after my head injury. The doctor said that might happen. Or memory loss . . . something like that. That'll explain why I've been acting weird lately, and why I went swimming with you in my undergarments. If I can say that, then I can face everyone tonight."

Phoenix focused his brown eyes on her. He looked troubled. "So why are you here?" he asked.

"What?"

"If you know what you have to do, why are you here? Why are you sobbing?"

"Because . . . I don't know why. Because I think I'm losing my mind," she railed. "I lost my mind as soon as I met you and I just wanted to talk to you about this and find out what you think."

He took her hands. "Courtney," he said

earnestly. "I don't think you're crazy. I think you're the sanest person I know."

Courtney sobbed and sniffed.

Phoenix kept staring at her. "Do you think what you did was wrong? Do you think taking off your clothes on a beautiful day and diving in the water was such a terrible thing to do?"

She didn't answer.

"Do you?"

"No," she finally replied, holding back a sob.

"Do you remember how we met?" he asked softly.

"Yes. Of course."

"Do you remember the rock poems I read to you while you were asleep?"

Finally, her tears stopped. "Yes, I remember. They were about changing seasons and the turning of the tide."

He touched her face. "So maybe you don't have memory loss, after all. Do you?"

She stared at him.

He brushed back his hair, then took her hand. "Do you remember how you fought me when I tried to make you stay in that hospital bed?"

She nodded.

"Do you remember how you argued with me when I tried to put you in the wheel-chair?"

"Yes."

His eyes never left her face. "Do you remember going to our dorm party, and letting me know you were there to break a rule or two?"

She knew that she would never, *ever* forget that.

"And do you remember the rope swing? Do you remember how it felt to have the wind against your body, how free and wonderful it was to swing so high and fall into the lake?"

She was beginning to smile. "Of course I remember all those things, Phoenix," she heaved. "But what does any of it matter now?"

He leaned forward and kissed her cheek. "If you're the same person that did all those things," he said pulling back to look at her, "then you're brave and you're strong. You were brave and strong then, and you're still brave and strong now. Unless you really have had a personality change."

Courtney stared at him, not quite sure what he was getting at.

"And you're honest, too," he said, smiling at her.

"Yes, I am," she admitted.

"Then you're the same Courtney you've always been. And you just have to go on being strong and brave and honest."

Courtney's tears had stopped completely. She finally knew what he meant. She stood up. "I have to leave," she said.

"I know." He stood up too. "Good luck. You know where I am if you want to find me again."

"Thank you, Phoenix."

She took a step toward the door, then turned around and reached out to him. She put one hand on his cheek, the other in his long hair, then she closed her eyes as she kissed him.

Phoenix wrapped his arms around her and held her so tight she could barely breath. Finally, he let her go, and Courtney knew she needed to be strong, brave, and honest.

Fourteen

"Where's Courtney Conner? She's supposed to give the welcome speech."

"Maybe she's not coming."

"Would you show up if everyone was passing around semi-nude pictures of you?"

"If I looked as good as Courtney, I might."

"Courtney is still my president and I still like her. I'm standing by her. I don't care what everyone else says."

"Well, maybe you don't care what people say, but I sure do."

"So do I."

The Tri Beta living room was decorated with streams of blue crêpe paper and balloons taped to the doorways and tables. Cardboard cutouts of U. of S. sporting events were tacked up, and a table held platters of cookies and cut-glass bowls of punch. Still, nothing looked festive to KC. She was wearing the expensive black dress she had splurged on for rush last fall, but suddenly black didn't seem elegant, so much as appropriate for a public hanging. The gossip made her sick to her stomach. All she could do was pray that Courtney would show up and things would calm down. The chatter continued.

"Has anyone checked Courtney's bedroom? Maybe she's just taking her time getting ready."

"Yeah. Maybe she's going to make a fashionably late entrance," a new Tri Beta pledge said hopefully.

A frat guy that KC suddenly recognized as Mark Geisslinger let out a dirty laugh. "Maybe she's getting ready to make her fashionable entrance in her underwear. Now that's something I'd sure like to see."

"Mark, shut up."

"Yeah, Mark. Go back to ODT."

"No way. I'm here for the show and I'm not leaving until the curtain comes down."

KC moved away from the nasty guffaws and wolf whistles. She was disgusted that so many Greek members were missing their own presidents' speeches in order to gloat and feel superior. Most of the Tri Beta girls were worried about Courtney and rooting for her, but people from the other houses simply wanted to watch Courtney suffer.

"I wouldn't blame her if she didn't show up," KC said to herself. She wandered through the crowded living room until she got to the bottom of the staircase. She looked up and thought of checking Courtney's bedroom again, but she had looked upstairs ten minutes before and Courtney hadn't been there.

Observing the welcome party, KC remembered how much she had longed for this moment. Since the first week of her arrival at U. of S., she had wanted to be a Tri Beta. Acceptance into the sisterhood meant that she was really breaking away from her hippie parents' lifestyle. But now that she had gotten into the elite sorority, she felt more strongly than ever that what really mattered were her friends.

KC stood alone until Diane suddenly scurried up with some other sisters. They all looked tense and very worried.

"Maybe *I* should make the welcome speech," Diane said, obviously at her wits' end. "We have to do something soon."

"I don't know," said another sister.

"Maybe she's never coming back," Diane pointed out. "I wouldn't blame her. But we also can't get along without her." Diane finally looked at KC. "Oh, KC. What are we going to do?"

KC didn't have an answer, but for the first time that night, she didn't need one. "Courtney," KC gasped.

A hush went over the living room and everyone turned to look at the front door. The loud gossipy voices turned to whispers.

"She's here."

"Oh my God."

"She looks kind of frazzled."

"I wonder what she's going to do."

The crowd parted, as Courtney slowly entered and began walking through the living room. She was wearing her old cardigan sweater over her silk dress. Her hair was wild, and her makeup was smeared, but she looked incredibly beautiful. Still, Courtney walked through the room was if she were stepping on eggs. She didn't look at anyone, until she neared the stairway and turned her head.

Courtney was no longer looking at the stairs, she was looking right into KC's eyes.

KC smiled. "I'm so glad to see you, Courtney," she said, trying to sound as supportive as she could.

Courtney glanced back to the crowd. She touched Diane's hand, then looked at KC again. "I'm glad to see you, too, KC," she nodded.

KC sat down as Courtney walked up to the front of the living room and held up her hands.

"Welcome . . . new Tri Beta pledges," Courtney began, her voice quaking and her eyes looking terrified. "Hello . . . everyone."

A few Tri Beta sisters applauded, but they were shushed. Then Mark wolf-whistled and KC shot him a fierce glare. Another Tri Beta pledge hit him in the shoulder.

Courtney cleared her throat and Diane rushed to get her a glass of water. By the time Diane returned from the kitchen, everyone was sitting down so they could get a good look.

Taking Diane's glass of water, Courtney swallowed. When she finished she saw that a Gamma sister on the living room couch was holding one of the much discussed swimming photos. Catching Courtney's eye, the girl quickly hid the photo. Giggles rose, then settled down again.

Courtney looked straight into the crowd. "Since there are so many non-Tri Betas here, I'd better introduce myself," she said. "My name is Courtney Conner. I am president of this sorority."

There was some polite applause, which quickly died down.

Courtney paused and looked around for Marielle. Relief crossed her face when she saw that Mark Geisslinger was alone. Courtney looked at KC again, and tried to wipe visions of Marielle out of her mind.

"Of course you all know why we're here tonight," Courtney said. She ignored the laughs and whispers that bubbled up again. "We're happy to have all our new pledges join us. We've always been . . . proud of our sisterhood, and we hope that you'll be proud, too.

The Tri Beta house is one of the most prestigious houses on the row."

"Not anymore," Mark said in an overly loud whisper.

More giggles erupted, along with more whispers and a few smutty laughs. Courtney ignored them. "Perhaps I should explain why I was late tonight," she announced.

"Good idea," someone yelled out.

Courtney tried to keep her head high. She wanted to be strong, but her resolve weakened. "I was in the hospital at the beginning of rush," she began. "I fell at Mill Pond and hit my head. I suffered a mild concussion. The doctors warned me to take it easy afterwards, but I wanted to get back to rush right away. They warned me that I could suffer. . . ."

Everyone was staring at her.

Courtney stopped. She was about to use memory loss and personality change as an excuse for her uncharacteristic behavior, when visions of Hosmer Lake started coming back with startling clarity. There was nothing to be ashamed of. Her life had changed in a wonderful way and *she* was responsible for that change, not some bump on her head. It made her happy and proud. If she lied about that now, she might as well throw her new freedom out the window.

No!!! Courtney thought.

Courtney took a step forward and began speaking again. "However, that doesn't have anything to do with tonight," she explained. "And really what I want to talk about is what happened afterwards. You see, I did a few things that some people might not think proper for a sorority president to do."

KC held her breath. She knew it was taking a lot of courage for Courtney to stand up for what she believed in, even if it meant being ousted from the sorority.

Courtney looked around the room. "I skipped a frat party at ODT, and I decided to visit my house's charity alone, rather than with the other girls. I went swimming at Hosmer Lake in my bra and panties. Someone took pictures of me, as many of you know."

People were leaning forward now and the room was very quiet.

"I'm glad I did all those things," Courtney went on. "Because I learned that although I'm part of a sorority, it doesn't mean I have to be a clone of my sisters. We're all individuals." She paused for air, then continued. "Our

Greek system has a lot of regulations and rules that define and keep us strong, but I think it's important to bend the rules sometimes. I even think it's important to make mistakes, and to forgive other people when they make mistakes, too. All of us in the Tri Betas need to be strong and honest and we need to take care of each other, not attack one another for being different. Most of all, we need to let our hair down once in a while." Courtney smiled. "We need to be able to have fun in this house and to learn what life is really about."

Courtney suddenly realized that she was finished. She gazed bravely into the crowd. "That's all," she said. "Except that I've always been proud to be a Tri Beta and I promise my new girls that I will make them feel proud, too."

She looked at KC, who began clapping her hands. This time the applause didn't die out. Diane joined in, then Lisa Jean McDermett began cheering and stamping her feet. After that Marcia Tabbert looked around and applauded.

"Bravo!" another person yelled from the back of the room.

"Yes, Courtney!"

"It's about time somebody loosened up around here!"

Soon the room exploded with cheers and fervent applause. Some of the pledges had jumped to their feet. A few Tri Beta sisters were crying. Only Mark Geisslinger and the other Greek Row onlookers who were expecting Courtney's downfall didn't join in the celebration.

Courtney moved into the crowd and smiled her most radiant smile. "Now, let's put on some music!" she cried, throwing back her head. "This is supposed to be a party!"

Someone loaded the Chuck Berry tape into the house cassette deck, and the living room began to rock and roll. Courtney wished that she could run back to the dorms and bring Phoenix over to dance with her. Instead, she caught little bits of gossip, as she walked around the room.

"She is *so* nervy. Can you believe it? I wish I'd pledged here instead of the Gammas."

"I would have pledged Tri Beta, but Courtney used to be so cold," said another girl, as she tossed Courtney's picture into the air. "I used to think she was stiff. But I guess that's changed."

"I'd say it's a definite change for the better."

Soon people were dancing and laughing. New visitors were wandering into the house, and Tri Beta pledges were venturing out to other open houses on the row.

Finally, Courtney found KC, who was helping load more refreshments onto the dining room table.

"Courtney!"

"KC."

"Hi, sister," KC said, giving Courtney a huge hug. "I made it, I guess."

"Hi, Tri Beta," Courtney answered with a smile. "I think I made it, too."

Here's a sneak preview of
Freshman Changes, the tenth
book in the dramatic story of
FRESHMAN DORM.

With a sigh, KC walked on alone. She trudged up the stairs of Langston House, walked across the front porch and through the old oak door. She looked around nervously, wondering whether anyone would notice she was wearing the same clothes as the night before. She knew how that would look to suspicious minds. Little would they know that she had spent the night at Winnie's.

She'd had a great guy in her life, but he was gone now. KC still hadn't figured out why Peter suddenly had turned on her. She knew she hadn't done anything wrong. There had to be something wrong with *him*. But what? And when would she be able to stop thinking about him all the time and stop feeling so much pain?

When KC reached the top of the stairs, she saw a lump of blue denim on the floor at the end of the hall. It looked as if it was in front of her room. Had someone left their laundry outside her door?

As KC got closer, she saw it wasn't laundry. It was a person in blue jeans and a blue jeans jacket, lying curled up in a ball. KC gasped when she realized who it was.

"Peter!" she said, half to herself, half-aloud.

Peter mumbled something and rolled over onto his back, still sleeping. KC gazed down at him tenderly. Was he having a bad dream? KC wanted to wrap him in her arms and tell him that everything would be okay.

Peter's eyelids started to flutter. Then he opened his eyes. As soon as he saw her, a smile lit up his face, and KC found herself smiling, too. Then she remembered that Peter had stood her up, given her the silent treatment, and now he dared to show up like a package on her doorstep? KC scowled.

Peter ran his hands through his already

messy, light brown hair. Then he stiffly rose to his feet. "I suppose you're wondering why I'm sleeping in your hallway," he said, looking down at his sneakers.

"Actually, Peter," KC said coolly, "I couldn't care less why you do anything. I'm surprised the janitor hasn't swept you away with the rest of the trash."

Peter pressed his lips together and shoved his hands into the pockets of his denim jacket. "Okay," he said. "I understand why you feel that way, and I don't blame you a bit. I also understand why you were gone all night. You've already found another boyfriend. But that's none of my business."

"How do you know I was gone all night?" KC asked.

Peter gestured at the floor by KC's door. "I slept here," he said.

"All night?" KC asked.

"Well, no, not exactly," Peter said. "The floor adviser kicked me out at midnight, so I slept on the grass outside your dorm. I came back in around eight o'clock this morning. I guess I fell asleep again."

KC couldn't bear the thought of how cold and uncomfortable Peter must have been all night. But she wasn't about to let him know that.

"That was stupid," she said. "What were you trying to do—catch pneumonia?"

"I wanted to talk to you," Peter said. "Not that I expect you to listen to me. But I wanted to explain why I never showed up at your sorority dance, so that even if things are over between us, at least you'll know I wasn't a complete jerk."

"Too late," KC said. "I've already reached that conclusion. Now, if you don't mind, would you please stop blocking my doorway? I'd like to go inside." KC tried to get around Peter, but he blocked her with his body. For several seconds, they stared each other down. KC tried to keep her expression fierce, but she could feel herself softening inside.

"Why didn't you just tell me in the dining commons when I tried to talk to you?" KC demanded. "Wouldn't that have been a whole lot more convenient than sleeping in my hall?"

"I didn't know then what I know now," Peter said. "You see, I thought you'd dumped me for that guy Sheldon. A girl on your floor told me she saw you together, and then I saw the two of you in my dorm, and it looked like you were all lovey-dovey, and I assumed the worst. Now I realize the problem wasn't you, or anything you did. It was *me*. I'm so insecure I just figured you'd throw me over for the next good-looking guy who came along. I guess I should have trusted you more."

"More?" KC demanded. "I don't think you trusted me at all."

"No," Peter admitted, looking down at his sneakers again. "And now I've got to suffer for it. I don't deserve you, and maybe what this proves is that you really are too good for me."

KC let her eyes rest on Peter's fine, silky hair. She looked at his faded jacket, rumpled jeans, and his scuffling, sneakered feet. "So you think I'm too good for you?" she asked in a stern voice.

Peter looked up again with such a mixture of pain, love, and despair that KC thought she was going to cry. "I know you are," he said.

"Do you want to know what I think?" KC asked.

Peter nodded, his brown eyes anxious.

"This is what I think," KC said, stepping forward and wrapping her arms around Peter. His denim jacket was still a little damp, so KC pulled it down off his shoulders and let it drop to the floor. Then she slid her fingers into the back pockets of his jeans and, standing on tiptoe, she closed her eyes and found his lips with her own.